SUGAR CREEK GANG

TEACHER
TROUBLE

Original title:
Shenanigans at Sugar Creek

Paul Hutchens

MOODY PRESS • CHICAGO

SHENANIGANS AT SUGAR CREEK
by PAUL HUTCHENS

Copyright 1947, by
Wm. B. Eerdmans Publishing Company

Assigned to Paul Hutchens, 1967

Moody Press Edition, 1969

ISBN 0-8024-4811-9

12 Printing/LC/Year 89 88 87 86 85

Printed in the United States of America

1

ONE TOUGH GUY in the Sugar Creek territory was enough to keep us all on the lookout all the time for different kinds of trouble. We'd certainly had plenty with Big Bob Till, who, as you maybe know, was the big brother of Little Tom Till, our newest gang member.

But when a new quick-tempered boy whose name was Shorty Long moved into the neighborhood and started coming to our school, and when Shorty and Bob began to chum around together, we never knew whether we'd get through even one day without something happening to start a fight, or get one of the gang into trouble with our teacher. On top of that, we had a new teacher, a man teacher at that, who didn't exactly know that most of us tried to behave ourselves most of the time.

Poetry, who is the barrel-shaped member of our gang, had made up a poem about our new teacher, whom not a one of us liked very well because of not wanting a new teacher when we'd liked our pretty woman teacher so well. This is the way the poem went:

3

> *The Sugar Creek Gang had the worst of teachers*
> *And "Black" his name was called,*
> *His round red face had the homeliest of features,*
> *He was fat and forty and bald.*

Poetry was always writing a new poem or always quoting one somebody else wrote.

Maybe it was a library book that was to blame for some of the trouble we had in this story though. I'm not quite sure, but the very minute my pal Poetry and I saw the picture in a book called *The Hoosier Schoolmaster,* we both had a very mischievous idea come into our minds, which we couldn't get out no matter how we tried.

This is the way it happened—Poetry and I were in his house, in fact, I was staying at his house all night one night, and just before we went to sleep, we sat up in his big bed for a while, looking at the picture which was a full-page glossy picture of a man schoolteacher up on the roof of a country schoolhouse, and he was holding a wide board across the top of the chimney. The schoolhouse's only door was open and a gang of tough-looking boys was tumbling out, along with a lot of smoke.

"Have you ever read the story?" I said to Poetry, and he said, "No, have you?" and when I said "No," we both read a part of it. The story was about a man teacher whose very bad boys in the school had locked him out of the building, and he had climbed up on the roof of the school and put a

4

board across the chimney and smoked them out just like a boy smokes a skunk out of a woodchuck den along Sugar Creek.

That put the idea in our heads, and it stayed there until a week or two after Christmas before it got us into trouble. Then just like a time bomb exploding, suddenly that innocent idea, which an innocent author had written in an innocent library book, exploded—and here is the story.

*　　*　　*

It was a swell Saturday afternoon at our house with bright sunlight on the snow and the weather just right for coasting. I was standing by our kitchen sink, getting ready to start wiping a big stack of dishes which my mom had just rinsed with steaming hot water out of the teakettle. I was just reaching for a drying towel when Mom said, "Better wash your hands first, Bill," which I had forgotten to do like I do once in a while. Right away I washed my hands with soap in our bathroom, came back and grabbed the towel off the rack by the range, and started in carefully wiping the dishes. I didn't exactly want to because the clock on our shelf said it was one o'clock, and the gang was supposed to meet on Bumblebee hill right that very minute with our sleds. We were going to have the time of our lives coasting, and rolling in the snow, and making huge balls and snowmen and everything.

5

You should have seen those dishes fly—that is, they *started* to!

"Be careful," Mom said, and meant it. "Those are my best dinner plates."

"I will," I said, and I was for a jiffy, but my mind wasn't anywhere near those fancy plates Mom was washing and I was wiping. In fact, there wasn't any sense in washing them anyway, 'cause they weren't the ones we had used that day at all. Why, they weren't even dirty! They'd been standing on the shelf in Mom's cupboard for several months without being used.

"I don't see why we have to wash them," I said, "when they aren't even dirty."

"We're going to have company for dinner tomorrow," Mom explained, "and we *have* to wash them."

"Wash them *before* we use them?" I said. It didn't make sense. Why that very minute the gang would be hollering and screaming and coasting down the hill and having a wonderful time.

"Certainly," Mom said. "We want them to sparkle so that when the table is set and the guests come in they'll see how beautiful they really are. See? Notice how dull this one is?" Mom held up one that hadn't been washed yet in her hot sudsy water nor rinsed in my hot clear water, nor wiped and polished with my dry clean towel, which Mom's tea towels always were anyway, Mom being an extra-clean housekeeper and couldn't help it because

6

her mother had been that way too—and being that kind of a housekeeper is contagious, like catching the measles or smallpox or the mumps or something boys don't like.

For some reason I remembered a part of a book I'd read, called *Alice in Wonderland,* and it was about a crazy queen who started to cry and say, "Oh! Oh! My finger's bleeding!" And when Alice, who was *in* Wonderland, told her to wrap her finger up or something, the queen said, "Oh no, I haven't pricked it yet," meaning it was bleeding *before* she had stuck a needle into it, which was a fairy story, and was crazy. So I said to Mom, "Seems funny to wash dishes *before* they're dirty—seems like a fairy story, like having your finger start bleeding before you stick a needle in it." I knew Mom had read *Alice in Wonderland* 'cause she'd read it to me herself when I was little.

But Mom was very smart. She said, with a mischievous sound in her voice, "That's a splendid idea. Let's pretend this is Bill Collins in Wonderland, and get the dishes done right away. Fairy stories are always interesting, don't you think?"

I didn't right then, but there wasn't any use arguing. In fact, Mom said it wasn't ever polite, so I quit and said, "Who's coming for dinner tomorrow?" I wondered if it might be some of the gang, and hoped it would be. I didn't know a one of the gang who would notice whether the dishes sparkled or not, although most of their moms probably would.

"Oh—a surprise," Mom said.

"Who?" I said. "My cousin Wally and his new baby sister?" Perhaps you know I had a homely, red-haired cousin named Walford who lived in the city, who had a new baby sister. Mom and Dad had been to see the baby, but I hadn't and didn't want to. And I certainly didn't exactly want to see Wally, but *would* like to see his crazy Airedale dog, and, if Wally *was* coming, I hoped he would bring the wire-haired dog along.

"It's a surprise," Mom said, and right that minute there was a whistle outside our house and at our front gate. I looked over the top of my stack of steaming dishes out through a clear place in the frosted window, and saw a fat-faced, barrel-shaped boy standing with one hand which had a red mitten on it, holding onto a sled rope, and he was lifting up the latch on our wide gate with the other red-mittened hand.

There was another boy there who I could tell without hardly looking was Dragonfly because he is spindle-legged and has large eyes like a dragonfly. Dragonfly had on a brand new cap with ear-muffs. Dragonfly was always getting the gang into trouble because he always was doing crazy things without thinking. He also was allergic to nearly everything and was always sneezing at the wrong

8

time, just when we were supposed to be quiet. Also, he was about the only one in the gang whose mother was superstitious, such as thinking it is bad luck if a black cat crosses the road in front of you, or good luck if you find a horseshoe and hang it above one of the doors in your house.

Just as Poetry had the latch of the wide gate lifted, I saw Dragonfly make a quick move, step with one foot on the iron pipe at the bottom of the gate's frame and give the gate a shove, and jump on with the other foot and ride on the gate while it was swinging open. This was something Dad wouldn't let me do, and which any boy shouldn't do, because if he keeps on doing it, it will make the gate sag and maybe drag on the ground.

Well, for a jiffy I forgot there was a window between me and the out-of-doors, and also that my mom was beside me, and also that my baby sister, Charlotte Ann, was asleep in Mom's bedroom in her baby bed. Without thinking I yelled real loud, "Hey, Dragonfly, you crazy goof! Don't do that!"

Right away I remembered Charlotte Ann was in the other room because Mom told me, and also Charlotte Ann woke up and made the kind of a noise a baby always makes when she wakes up and doesn't want to.

Just that second the gate Dragonfly was on was as wide open as it could go, and Dragonfly who didn't have a very good hold with his hands—and the gate being icy anyway—slipped off and went sprawling head over heels into a snowdrift in our yard.

It was a funny sight, but not very funny 'cause I heard my dad's great big voice calling from our barn, yelling something that sounded like he sounds when somebody has done something he shouldn't and is supposed to quit quick, or he'd be sorry.

I made a dive for our back door, swung it open, and with one of my Mom's good plates still in my hands, and without my hat on, I rushed out on our back boardwalk and yelled to Poetry and Dragonfly, and said, "I'll be there in about an hour! I've got to finish tomorrow's dishes first! Better go on down the hill and tell the gang I'll be there in maybe an hour or two," which is what is called sarcasm.

And Poetry yelled, "We'll come and help you!"

But it wasn't a good idea, 'cause the kitchen door was still open and Mom heard me and also heard Poetry and said to me, "Bill Collins, come back in here. The very idea! I can't have those boys coming in with all that snow. I've just scrubbed the floor!" That is why they didn't come in, and also why barrel-shaped Poetry and spindle-legged Dragonfly started building a snowman right in our front yard, while they waited for me and Mom to finish.

Pretty soon I was done though, and I grabbed my coat from its hook in the corner of the kitchen, pulled my hat on my red head, with the earmuffs tucked inside because it wasn't a very cold day, but was warm enough for the snow to pack good and for making snowballs and snowmen and everything. I put on my boots at the door, said good-bye to Mom and went swishing out through the snow to Poetry and Dragonfly. I could already hear the rest of the gang yelling down on Bumblebee hill, so I grabbed my sled rope which was right beside our back door, and the three of us went as fast as we could through our gate.

My Dad was there, looking at the gate to see if Dragonfly had been too heavy for it, and just as we left, he said, "Never ride on a gate, boys, if you want to live long."

His voice was kind of fierce, like it sometimes is, and he was looking at Dragonfly; then he looked at me and winked, and I knew he wasn't mad but still didn't want any boy to be dumb enough to ride on our gate again.

"Yes sir, Mr. Collins," Dragonfly said politely, grabbing his sled rope and starting on the run across the road to a place in the rail fence where I always climbed through on my way to the woods.

"Wait a minute!" Dad said, and we waited.

His big bushy eyebrows were straight across, so I knew he liked us all right. "What?" I said.

He said, "You boys know, of course, that your new teacher, Mr. Black, is going to keep on teaching the Sugar Creek School—that the board can't

11

ask him to resign just because the boys in the school liked their other teacher better, nor because he has had to punish several of them with old-fashioned beech switches."

Imagine my dad saying such things, just when we had been thinking about having a lot of fun.

"Yes sir," I said to Dad, remembering the beech switches behind the teacher's desk.

"Yes sir," Poetry said politely.

"Yes sir," Dragonfly yelled to him from the rail fence where he was already halfway through.

We all hurried through the fence, and yelling and running and panting, we dragged our sleds through the woods to Bumblebee hill to where the gang was yelling and having a lot of fun.

Well, we all coasted for a long time. Even Little Tom Till, the red-haired, freckled-faced little brother of Big Bob Till who was Big Jim's worst enemy, was there. Time flew faster than anything, when all of a sudden Circus, who had rolled a big snowball down the hill, said, "Let's make a snowman—let's make Mr. Black"—which sounded like more fun, so we all started in, not knowing that Circus was going to make a comic snowman, the most ridiculous-looking snowman I'd ever seen, and not knowing something else very exciting which I'm going to tell you about just as quick as I can.

2

Iᴛ ᴡᴀѕ the craziest snowman I had ever seen when we got through. It didn't have any legs because we had to use a very large snowball for its foundation, but it had another even larger snowball for its stomach because our new teacher was round in the middle, especially in front, and it had a smaller head. Circus, whose idea it was to make it funny, had dashed home to our house and gotten some corn silk out of our crib and had made hair for the man's head, putting it all around the sides of the top of its head, but not putting any in the middle of the top, nor in the front, so it looked like an honest-to-goodness bald-headed man. Then, while different ones of us were putting a row of buttons on his coat, which were black walnuts which we stuck into the snow in his stomach, Circus and Dragonfly disappeared, leaving only Poetry and Little Jim and Little Tom Till and me. That was all the rest of the gang that was there because Big Jim had had to go with his dad that afternoon to take a load of cattle to the city.

*   *   *

I was sitting down on my sled which was crosswise on the top of Little Jim's, which was crosswise on the top of Poetry's, making my seat just about knee-high. Our snowman was at the bottom of the hill and not very far from us was a beech tree. Little Jim was standing there under its low-hanging branches, looking up into it, like he was thinking something very important which he nearly always is. Little Jim was the best Christian in the gang and was always thinking and sometimes saying something he had learned in church or that his parents taught him from the Bible. There were nearly half of the leaves still on the tree in spite of its being winter and nearly every other tree in the woods was as bare as Old Mother Hubbard's cupboard. It was a beech tree and that kind of a tree nearly always keeps a lot of its old frost-bitten brown leaves on nearly all winter, and only drops them off in the spring when the new leaves start to come and push them off.

It was the same tree where one summer day there had been a big old mother bear and her cub. All of a sudden while I was sitting there on my stack of sleds I was remembering that fight we'd had with the old fierce mother bear. I guessed maybe Little Jim was remembering it also. Everything was so quiet, I said to Little Jim, "I bet you're thinking about how you killed a bear right there."

Little Jim, who had his stick which he always carried with him, said, "Nope, something else."

Poetry spoke up from where he was standing beside Mr. Black's snow statue, and said, "I'll bet you're thinking about the little cub which you had for a pet after you killed the bear."

Little Jim took a swipe with his stick at the trunk of the tree, and I noticed that his stick went kerwhack right on some initials on the tree which said, W. J. C., which meant "William Jasper Collins," which is my full name, only nobody ever calls me by the middle name except my dad, who calls me that only when he doesn't like me or when I'm supposed to have done something I shouldn't. Then Little Jim said to Poetry, just as his stick kerwhammed the initials, "Nope, something else." Then he whirled around and started making tracks that looked like rabbit tracks in the snow with his stick, and Tom Till spoke up and said, "I'll bet you're thinking about the fight we had that day."

It was in that fight that I licked little red-haired Tom Till, who with his big brother Bob had belonged to the other gang. But now Little Tom's parents lived in our neighborhood and Tom had joined the gang, and also went to our Sunday school, and was a swell little guy; but Bob was still a tough guy and hated Big Jim and all of us, and we never knew when he was going to start some new trouble in the Sugar Creek territory.

15

"Well," I said to Little Jim, who was looking up into the tree again like he was still thinking something important, "what *are* you thinking about?"

And he said, "I was just thinking about all the leaves, and wondering why they didn't fall off like the ones on the maple trees do. Don't they know they're dead?"

I looked at the tree Little Jim was looking at, and it was the first time I'd noticed that the beech tree still had nearly every one of its leaves on it. They were very brown, even browner than some of the maple and walnut tree leaves had been when they'd all fallen off last fall.

"How could they know they're dead, if they *are* dead?" Poetry said.

Just that second I heard Circus and Dragonfly coming up from the direction of the bayou, which was down pretty close to Sugar Creek itself. Circus had his knife and was just finishing trimming a small branch he had in his hand. Dragonfly had a long fierce-looking switch in one of his hands, and was swinging it around and saying loud and fierce, "All right, Bill Collins, you can take a licking for throwing that snowball—take that—and that—and that—" Dragonfly was making fierce swings with his switch and grunting every time he swung.

I knew what he was thinking about—the snowball I'd thrown in our school yard that week, which

16

had accidentally hit our new teacher right in the middle of the top of his bald head.

Well, in a jiffy, Circus had both those switches stuck into the snowman, right where his right hand was supposed to be. Then he reached into his pocket and pulled out an ear of corn and, as quick as anything, began to shell it, shoving handfulls of the big yellow kernels into his pocket at the same time. A jiffy later, all that was left was a long red corncob, which he broke in half and stuck one of the halves into the snowman's face for a nose.

Then, also as quick as anything, he took the other half of the red corncob and with his knife made a hole in its side near the bottom, took a small stick out of his pocket, stuck it into the cob! "What on earth?" I said.

But he said, "All right, everybody, shut your eyes," which we wouldn't, so we watched him finish what he was doing, which was making a pipe for the snowman to smoke. A jiffy later it was sticking into the snowman's snow face right under his nose —a corncob pipe. It looked very funny, and for a jiffy we all laughed, all except Little Jim who just giggled a little.

We all stood back and looked at it, and it was the funniest looking snowman I'd ever seen. Brown hair all around his head, and none in the middle of the top or the front, and a big red nose, and a corncob pipe sticking out at an angle, and black walnuts for buttons on his coat, and a couple of fierce-looking switches in his hand. Also there were two thin corn silk eyebrows that curled up a little.

"There's only one thing wrong with it," Poetry said, in his ducklike voice, standing beside me and squinting up at the ridiculous looking snowman.

"What?" I said, thinking how perfect it was.

"You can't tell who it is supposed to be. It needs some extra identification."

"It's perfect," I said, and looked at Little Jim to see if he didn't think the same thing. But he was looking up into the beech tree again, like he was still thinking about something mysterious and wasn't interested in an ordinary snowman.

I looked toward Dragonfly and he was listening toward a half-dozen little cedar trees in the direction of the bayou, like he was either seeing or hearing something, which he thought he was, for right that second he said, "Psst, gang, quiet! I think I saw something move over there—sh! Don't look now, or he'll—"

We all looked, of course, but didn't see anything, although I had a funny feeling inside of me which was, *What if it's Mr. Black watching us? What if all of a sudden he should come walking out from behind those cedar trees and see the snowman we've made of him, and what if he'd decide to use one or two of the switches on us?* Not a one of us was sure he didn't like us well enough to do that to us.

18

Poetry spoke up then and said, "I say it's not quite perfect. There's one thing wrong with it, and I'm going to fix that right this very minute." With that remark, he pulled off one of his red mittens, shoved one of his fat hands inside his coat pocket, pulled something out, and started to shuffle toward Mr. Black's snow statue. I could hardly believe my eyes at what I saw, but there it was as plain as day, a red, cloth-bound book with gold letters on it which said, *The Hoosier Schoolmaster*. I knew right away it was the book he and I had seen and had read part of in his library one night, that part especially where the tough gang of boys in the story had caused the teacher a lot of trouble, and had locked him out of the schoolhouse. Then the teacher, who had been very smart, had climbed up on top of the school and put a flat board across the top of the chimney. And the smoke, which couldn't get out of the chimney, had poured out of the stove inside, and all the tough gang of boys had been smoked out.

"What are you going to do?" I said to Poetry.

He said, "Nothing," and right away was doing it, which was sticking two sticks in the snowman's stomach side by side and then opening *The Hoosier Schoolmaster* to the place where there was the picture of the teacher on the roof, and laying the book flat open across the two sticks.

"There you are, sir," Poetry said, talking to the snowman. "The Hoosier Schoolmaster himself."

Then Poetry made a bow as low as he could, he being so fat he grunted every time he stooped over very far.

Well, it was funny, and most of us laughed. Circus scooped up a snowball and started to throw it at it, but we all stopped him because of not wanting to have all our hard work spoiled in a few minutes. Besides, Poetry suddenly wanted to take a picture of it, and his camera was at his house which was away down past the sycamore tree and the cave, where we all wanted to go for a while to see Old Man Paddler. So we decided to leave Mr. Black out there by himself at the bottom of Bumblebee hill until we came back later, which we did.

"He ought to have a hat on," Dragonfly said. "He'll catch his death of cold with his bald head."

"Or he might get stung on the head by a bumblebee," Circus said.

Little Jim spoke up all of a sudden and said, like he was almost mad at us, "Can anybody help it that he gets bald? My dad's beginning to lose some of his hair on top—" Then he grabbed his stick which he had leaned up against the beech tree for a jiffy, and struck very fiercely at a tall brown mullein stalk that was standing there in a little open space, and the seeds scattered in every direction, one of them hitting me hard right on my freckled face just below my right eye, and stung like everything. Then Little Jim started running as fast as he could go in the direction of the sycamore tree, like he had been mad at us for something we'd done wrong.

In fact, when he said that, I felt a kind of sickish feeling inside of me, like maybe I *had* done something wrong. I grabbed my stick and started off on the run after Little Jim, calling out to the rest of the gang to hurry up, and saying, "Last one to the sycamore tree is a cow's tail." In a jiffy we were running and jumping and diving around bushes and trees and leaping over snow-covered brush piles toward the old sycamore tree and the mouth of the cave which comes out at the other end in the cellar of Old Man Paddler's cabin.

3

OF COURSE everybody knows about Old Man
Paddler, the kindest long-whiskered old man who
ever lived, and the best friend the Sugar Creek
Gang ever had. He lived up in the hills above Sugar
Creek, and almost every week the gang went up to
see him—sometimes in the summer-time we went
nearly every day. We went in the winter too because
he lived all by himself and we had to go up to take
him things which our moms were always cooking
for him. Also, we had to be sure he didn't get sick
'cause there wouldn't be anybody there to take care
of him or call the doctor for him because he didn't
have a telephone.

After a little while we were tired of running so
fast, so we slowed down, it being easier to be a cow's
tail than to get all out of breath. Poetry and I were
side by side most of the time with Little Jim walking
along behind us and with Little Tom Till and Circus
and Dragonfly swishing on ahead of us. Once when
little red-haired Tom and Little Jim were beside
each other behind Poetry and me, I heard Little
Jim say to Tom, "Mom says for you to be ready

22

a little early tomorrow morning because the choir has to practice the anthem again before they sing."

I knew what Little Jim was talking about 'cause his folks stopped at Tom's house every Sunday morning about nine o'clock, and Little Tom got in and rode to Sunday school with them in their big maroon and gray car. Little Jim's pretty mom was the pianist at our church, and always had to be on time. Little Jim's words came out kind of jerkily like he was doing something that made him short of breath while he talked. I turned around quick to see and, sure enough, he was shuffling along, making rabbit tracks with his stick, and saying his words with every punch of his stick into the snow.

Little Tom answered by saying, "O de koke," which is the same as saying, "Okey doke," which means "OK" which is what most anybody says when he means "all right," meaning Tom Till would be ready early, and that when Little Jim's folks came driving up to their front gate tomorrow, Little Tom, with his best clothes on, would come running out of their dilapidated old unpainted house, carrying his New Testament, which Old Man Paddler had bought for him. Then they'd all swish away together to Sunday school.

Then I heard Little Jim ask something else which showed what a grand little guy he was. "S'pose maybe your mother would like to go with us too?"

"My mother would *like* to go with us," Tom said

to Little Jim, "but she doesn't have any clothes that are good enough." And knowing the reason why was because her husband drank up nearly all the money he made in the Sugar Creek beer taverns, and also drank whiskey which he bought in the liquor store—knowing that, I felt my teeth gritting hard and I took a fierce swing with the stick I was carrying, at a little maple tree beside me. I socked that tree so fierce with my stick that my hands stung so bad they were almost numb; the stick broke in the middle and one end of it flew ahead to where Circus and Dragonfly were and nearly hit them.

"Hey, you!" Dragonfly yelled back toward us. "What you trying to do—kill us?"

"What on earth!" Circus yelled back to me, and I stood looking at the broken end of the rest of the stick in my hand, then turned like a flash and whirled around and threw it as hard as I could straight toward another tree about twenty feet away. That broken stick hit the tree right in the center of its trunk with a loud whack.

I didn't answer them in words at all. I was so mad at Tom's dad and at beer and whiskey and stuff.

But I couldn't waste all my temper on something I couldn't help, so I kept still and we all went on to the cave and went in, following its long narrow passageway clear through until we came to the big wooden door which opened into Old Man Paddler's cellar. As soon as we got there, Circus, who was always the leader of our gang when Big Jim wasn't with us, stopped us and made us keep still. Then he knocked on the door—three knocks, then two, then three more, then two, which was the code the gang always used when we came so Old Man Pad- dler would know it was us.

If he was home, he would call down and say in his quavering old voice, "Who's there?" and we'd answer, and right away we'd hear his trapdoor in the floor of his house open, and hear his steps com- ing down his stairway and hear him lift the big wooden latch that held the door shut. Then when he'd see us, he'd say, "Well, well, well, well, the Sugar Creek Gang—" Then he'd name everyone of us by our nicknames, and say, "Come in, boys, we'll have some sassafras tea," which all of us, espe- cially Little Jim, liked so very much.

Everything was quiet when Circus knocked three times, then two, then three, and then two again, while we all waited and listened. There was always something kind of spooky about that knock and, being in a cave, I always felt a little queer until I heard the old man's voice answer us. In fact, I al- ways felt creepy until we got inside the cabin and the trapdoor was down again.

We all stood there, outside that big wooden door, waiting for Old Man Paddler to call down to us, but there wasn't a single sound, so Circus knocked again three times, then two, then three, and then two again, and we all waited. Except for my little pocket flashlight which my dad had given me for Christmas, we didn't have any light, and we couldn't waste the battery by keeping it on all the time. So I turned it off, but it felt so spooky with it off and nobody answering Circus's knock that I turned it on again just as Dragonfly who was always hearing things first, said, "Psst!" which meant "I heard something mysterious! Everybody keep still a minute," which we did. And then as plain as day I heard it myself, an old man's voice talking. It was high-pitched and quavering, and kind of sadlike, like he was begging somebody to do something for him.

We were all as quiet as mice, not a one of us moving or hardly breathing. I couldn't hear a word the old man was saying, but he sounded like he needed help. I remembered how we'd all saved his life two different times—once when a robber had tied him up and he'd have starved if we hadn't found him, and another time when he'd fallen down his cellar steps in the wintertime and his fire had gone out. We had started a fire for him with punk, using the thick lenses of his reading glasses for a magnifying glass, which any boy can do if he can get some real dry punk and a magnifying glass. First you focus the red hot light which shines from the sun through the magnifying glass right on the punk until it makes a little smoking live coal, then you hold a piece of dry paper against the red glow on the punk, and blow and blow until all of a sudden there will be a real flame of fire.

Say, when I heard Old Man Paddler half talking and half crying up there in his cabin, I got a very queer feeling inside of me.

"Quick!" Circus said, "He's in trouble. Let's go in and help him." Circus gave a shove on the door, turning the latch at the same time, but the door wouldn't budge.

"It's barred," Poetry said, and I remembered the heavy bar on the inside which the old man always dropped into place whenever he was inside.

"Sh! Listen!" Little Jim said, and we shushed and listened.

Say, that little guy had his ear pressed up real close to a crack in the door, and in the light of my flashlight which I didn't shine straight on his face because it might blind him, I could see that his eyes had a very faraway look in them, like he was thinking something important and maybe in his mind's eyes was seeing something even more important.

"What is it?" I said to him.

He said, "Don't worry, he's all right. He doesn't need our help—here, listen yourself."

I did, and right away I knew Little Jim was right. For this is what I heard the old man saying in his quavering, high-pitched voice, "And please, You're the best Friend I ever had, letting me live all these long years, taking care of me, keeping me well and strong and happy most of the time. But I'm getting lonesome now, getting older every day, getting so I can't walk without a cane, and I can't stand the cold weather anymore, and I know it won't be long before I'll have to move out of this crippled-up old house and come to live with You in a new place. I'll be awful glad to see Sarah again, and my boys. And that reminds me—please bless the boys who live and play along Sugar Creek—all of 'em—Big Jim, Little Jim, Circus, Dragonfly, Poetry, Bill Collins—"

I knew what the kind man was doing all right, 'cause I'd seen and heard him do it many a time in our little white church, and also I'd seen him doing it once down on his knees behind the old sycamore tree all by himself. When I heard him mention my name, I gulped, and some crazy tears got into my eyes and into my voice. I had to swallow to keep from choking out a word that would have let the gang know that I was about to cry. Like a flash I thought of something and I whirled around and grabbed Little Tom Till and shoved his ear down to the crack in the door and put my ear just above his so I could hear too, and this is what the old man was saying up there in the cabin, "And also bless the new member of the gang, Tom Till, whose father is an atheist and spends his money on liquor and gambling. O God, how can John Till expect his boys to keep from turning out to be criminals? Bless his boy, Bob, whose life has been so bent and twisted by his father. And bless the boys' poor mother, who hasn't had a chance in life. Lord, You know she'd go to church and be a Christian if John would let her. And please—"

That was as far as I got to listen right that minute 'cause I heard somebody choke and gulp and all of a sudden Little Tom Till was sniffling like he had tears in his eyes and in his voice. Then that little guy, who was the grandest little guy who ever had a drunkard for a father, started to sob aloud like he was heartbroken and couldn't help himself.

I got the strangest feeling inside of me like I do when anybody cries, and I wanted to help him stop crying and didn't know what to do.

"'Smatter?" Dragonfly said.

Tom said, "I want to go home!"

"'Smatter?" Circus said, "Are you sick?"

"Yeah, what's the matter?" Poetry's ducklike voice squawked.

But Little Jim was a smart little guy and he said, "He doesn't feel well. Let's all take him home."

"I'll go b-b-by m-m-myself," Little Tom said, and started back into the cave.

But I knew it was too dark for him to see, so I grabbed his arm and pulled him back. "We'll all go with you."

29

"But we wanted to see Old Man Paddler," Dragonfly said. "What's the use to go home? I want some sassafras tea."

"Keep still," I said, "Tom's sick. He ought to go home." I knew Little Tom was terribly embarrassed, and that he'd be like a little scared rabbit if we took him into Old Man Paddler's cabin now.

We must have made a lot of noise talking 'cause right that minute I heard Old Man Paddler's voice up there calling down to us, "Wait a minute, boys! I'll be right down."

Well, it would have been impolite to run away now, and so I whispered to Tom, "Me and Little Jim are the only ones who heard him praying—and we—we like you anyway." I gave Tom a kind of fierce half a hug around his shoulder, just as I heard Old Man Paddler's trapdoor in the floor of his house opening, and a shaft of light came in through the crack in the door right in front of us. In a jiffy our door would open too, and we'd see that kind, long-whiskered old man, with his twinkling gray eyes, and pretty soon we'd all climb up the cellar steps and be inside his warm cabin with a fire crackling in his fireplace and with the teakettle on the stove for making sassafras tea, and the old man would be telling us a story about the Sugar Creek of long ago.

All of a sudden I got the strangest warm feeling inside of me, and I felt so good, something just bubbled up in my heart. It was the queerest feeling, and made me feel good all over, 'cause right that second one of Little Tom's arms reached out and gave me a very awkward half a hug real quick, like he was very bashful or something, but like he was saying, "You're my best friend, Bill—I'd lick the stuffin's out of the biggest bum in the world for you, in fact I'd do *anything*."

But his arm didn't stay more'n just time enough for him to let it fall to his side again, but I knew he liked me a lot and it was a wonderful feeling.

Right that second I heard the old man lift the bar on the big wooden door and push it open. A real bright light came in and shone all over all of us, and the old man said, "Well, well, well, well, the Sugar Creek Gang! Come on in, boys, we'll have a party."

A jiffy later we were all inside his cellar and scrambling up his cellar steps into his warm cabin.

4

IT DIDN'T TAKE more'n several jiffies for all of us to be inside that old-fashioned cabin where there was a crackling fire in his fireplace and another fire roaring in his kitchen stove and where there was a teakettle singing like everything, meaning that pretty soon we'd have some sassafras tea. In fact, as soon as the trapdoor was down and we were all sitting or standing or half lying down on his couch and on chairs, the old man put some sassafras chips from sassafras tree roots into a pan on the stove and poured boiling water on it, and let it start to boil. Almost right away the water began to turn as red as the chips themselves and Little Jim's eyes grew very bright as he watched the water boil.

One of the first things I noticed when I looked around the room a little was the old man's Bible which was open to the Sunday school lesson, like maybe he'd been studying, getting ready for church tomorrow. I knew it was tomorrow's lesson 'cause at our house we had already studied the same lesson two or three times because Mom and Dad always started to study next week's lesson a whole week ahead of time so, as Dad says, "Different ideas will come popping into our heads all week long even while we're working or studying or something." I knew Little Jim's parents always started studying their lessons the first thing in the week also, and maybe that was why that little guy was always thinking of so many things that were important.

From where I was sitting, I could look through a clear place in the old man's kitchen window which didn't have any frost on it, and I could see the shadow the smoke was making which was coming out of the chimney, and the longish darkish shadow was moving up the side of the old man's woodshed out there, and on up the slant of the snow-covered roof, making me think of a great big long darkish worm twisting and squirming and crawling up a stick in the summertime. There must have been almost a foot of snow on the roof of that woodshed, I thought, and that reminded me of the snowman at the bottom of Bumblebee hill. And when I noticed that the shadows of the trees out there were getting very long it meant that it wouldn't be long till the sun went down and, if Poetry and I were to get a good picture of Mr. Black's snow statue, we'd have to hurry.

Old Man Paddler suddenly spoke up and said to us, looking especially at me, "One of you boys want to take the water pail and go down to the spring and get a pail of fresh water?"

I didn't exactly want to because it was very warm in the cabin and would be very cold out there. But when Little Jim piped up and said, "Sure, I'll do it," I all of a sudden said the same thing. Little Jim and I were out there less than a jiffy, with the old man's empty pail in one of my hands, and were galloping along through the snow toward the spring, which was right close to a big spreading beech tree which, like the one at the bottom of Bumblebee hill, still had most of its old brown leaves on.

We filled the pail real quick with the sparkling, very cold water, and hurried back to the cabin. I had started to open the door when Little Jim said, "Wait a minute, I want to see something." He swished around quick and went back down the path toward the spring, and turned around again and looked up toward the chimney of the old man's cabin. He squinted his eyes to keep the sun from blinding them and looked and looked, then he looked away in the direction of the woodshed, and I wondered what in the world that little guy was thinking.

"'Smatter?" I said.

He said, "Nothing—there's certainly a lot of snow on the roof of that woodshed, and there isn't any on the old man's cabin. How come?" Then he socked a stump with his stick, and came lickety-sizzle to the door and opened it for me to go in with the pail of water.

Well, as soon as we got through with our sassafras tea, which Little Jim said tasted like a very sweet hot lollipop, we all scrambled around in the old man's cabin getting ready to go home. If it had been in the summertime, we would have gone home the long way around, following the old wagon trail, and then we'd have taken a shortcut through the swamp, and maybe stopped at the big mulberry tree and climbed up into it and helped ourselves to the biggest, ripest mulberries that grew anywhere along Sugar Creek. But it wasn't summer, so we took the shortcut, going through the cave to the sycamore tree, where most of us separated and went in different directions, all except Poetry and me, who were going to get his camera and take a picture of Mr. Black's snow statue, his parents having bought a new camera for him at Christmas.

* * *

"Well, well," Poetry's mother said to us when we stopped beside their big maple tree, and I waited a jiffy for him to go in the house and get the camera, "where have you boys been? I've been phoning all over for you, Leslie." She meant she had been phoning all over for Poetry, *Leslie* being the name which his parents used and which he had to use himself when he signed his name in school. But he would rather be called Poetry.

" 'Smatter?" Poetry asked his kind of round-shaped mom, "Didn't I do my chores, or something?"

Then Poetry's mother startled us by saying, "We've had company. Mr. Black was here. He just left a minute ago."

I had a queer feeling start creeping up my spine.

"What did he want—I mean, where did he go? Where'd you tell him we were?" Poetry and I both said at the same time only in different words, but with probably the same scared feeling inside, and thinking, *What if she told him we were playing over on Bumblebee hill and he went there?*

"He didn't seem to want anything in particular. He was out exercising his horse. Such a beautiful big brown saddle horse!" Poetry's mother said. "And such a very beautiful saddle. He looks very stunning in his brown leather jacket and riding boots."

"What did he want?" Poetry said again, taking the words right out of my mind.

Poetry's mom said, "'Nothing in particular. He said he wanted to get acquainted with the parents of his boys."

I looked at Poetry and he looked at me, and he said to his mom, "He's too heavy for the horse."

His mother looked at Poetry who was also heavy and said, "Too much blackberry pie, I suppose. You boys want a piece?"

Poetry's face lit up, and he said, "We'll take a piece apiece," which we did.

Then I said to him all of a sudden, "The sun'll be shining on Mr. Black. If we want to get his picture, we'll have to hurry!"

"Shining on whom?" Poetry's mom asked.

Poetry said, "The sun is shining in through the window on my blackberry pie," and winked at me. His mom went into their parlor to answer the phone which was ringing.

Poetry finished his pie at the same time, slithered out of his chair and went upstairs to his room to get his camera, just as I heard his mother say into their telephone, "Why yes, Mrs. Mansfield, we do—certainly, I'll send Leslie right over with it right away —oh, that's all right—no, he won't mind, I'm sure."

It sounded like an ordinary conversation any mother might have with any ordinary neighbor. I'd heard my mom say something like that many a time, the only difference being she would say, "Why yes, Mrs. So-and-So, we have it. I'll send Bill over with it right away—oh, that's all right—no, he won't mind, I'm sure," which I hardly ever did anymore because my dad wouldn't let me. I was always running an errand for some neighbor who didn't have any boys in the family, which is what boys are for.

I was wondering where Poetry had to go, with what and why, when Poetry's mom called up the stairs to him and said, "Leslie, will you bring down *The Hoosier Schoolmaster,* and you and Bill take it over to Mrs. Mansfield."

I heard Poetry gasp and call back down, "Get *what*?"

"The Hoosier Schoolmaster!" his mom called up. "It's on the second shelf in your library—it's a red book with gold lettering on it." Then Mrs. Thompson said to me, "Having a new gentleman teacher in the community has made everybody interested in that very interesting book, so Mrs. Mansfield is going to review it for the Literary Society next Wednesday night."

Then Poetry's mom called up to him and asked, "Find it, Leslie?" which of course he hadn't and couldn't, anyway not upstairs, 'cause right that minute it was lying open on two sticks stuck into Mr. Black's stomach at the bottom of Bumblebee hill. For some reason it didn't seem as if we wanted to tell Mrs. Thompson where it was, but it looked like we were in for it.

We couldn't come right out and tell her where the book was, 'cause she was like most of the other parents in Sugar Creek territory. She thought Mr. Black, who rode a fine horse and wore a brown leather jacket and riding boots and who could smile politely and tip his hat whenever he saw a Sugar Creek Gang mother, was a very fine gentleman, and certainly didn't know what a hard time the gang had been having with him.

Just that second Poetry called down and said, "Bill and I'll take it to her."

38

The gang didn't know Mrs. Mansfield very well because she was a new person in the Sugar Creek territory and didn't have any boys. She was more interested in society than any of the gang's moms and was always reading important books because it maybe made her seem more important if she knew the names of all the important books and who wrote them.

Poetry came downstairs with his camera, coming down in a big hurry and saying to me in a business-like voice, "Let's get going, Bill," and made a dive for the door so his mom wouldn't see he didn't have *The Hoosier Schoolmaster,* not wanting her to ask where it was, so he wouldn't have to tell her.

Both Poetry and I were out-of-doors in a jiffy and the door was half shut behind us when Poetry's mother said, "Hadn't we better wrap it up, Leslie— just in case you might accidentally drop it?"

"I promise you, I won't drop it," Poetry said, "besides we want to hurry. I want to take a picture of something before the sun gets too far down. Come on, Bill, hurry up!"

I hurried after him, both of us running fast out through their backyard in the direction of Bumble-bee hill.

But Poetry's mother called to us from the back door and said, "Where are you going? Mrs. Mansfield doesn't live in *that* direction."

Poetry and I stopped and looked at each other.

All of a sudden we knew we were caught, so Poetry said to me, "What'll we tell her?"

And remembering something my dad had taught me to do when I was caught in a trap, I said all of a sudden, quoting my dad, "Tell her the truth."

Poetry scowled. "You tell her," he said.

I did, saying, "Mrs. Thompson, the gang had *The Hoosier Schoolmaster* this afternoon, and we left him—I mean *it*—down on Bumblebee hill. We have to go there first to get it." All of a sudden I felt fine inside, and knew that Dad was right. Poetry's mom might not like to hear exactly where the book was right that very minute, and it didn't seem exactly right to tell her. So when she didn't ask me, I didn't tell her.

Poetry's mother must have understood her very mischievous boy though and didn't want to get him into a corner, for she said, "Thank you for telling me. Now I can phone Mrs. Mansfield that it will take a little longer for you to get there with the book—and, by the way, if you see Mr. Black tell him about next Wednesday night — you probably will see him. I told him you boys were over on Bumblebee hill and how to get there. He seemed to want to see you."

Poetry and I both yelled back to her, saying, "You told him *what!*" Without another word or waiting to hear what she said, we started like lightning as fast as we could go, straight for Sugar Creek and Bumblebee hill, wondering if by taking a short-cut we could get there before Mr. Black did. In my mind's eye, I could see Poetry, *if* we got there first, making a dive for *The Hoosier Schoolmaster* on the snowman. And I could see myself, making a leap for the man's head, and knocking it completely off, I could see it go rolling the rest of the way down the hill with its corn-silk hair getting covered with snow—also I could see Mr. Black in his brown riding jacket and boots, on his great big saddle horse, riding up right about the same minute.

What if we don't get there first? I thought. *What if we don't? It will be awful! Absolutely terrible!* And Poetry must have been thinking the same thing 'cause, for once in his life, in spite of his being barrel-shaped and very heavy and never could run very fast, I had a hard time keeping up with him.

5

ALL THE TIME while Poetry and I were running through the snowy woods, squishety-sizzle, zip-zip-zip, crunch, crunch, crunch, I could see in my mind's eye our new teacher's big beautiful brown saddle horse, prancing along in the snow toward Bumblebee hill, carrying his heavy load just as easy as if it wasn't anything. Right that very minute maybe the horse would be standing and pawing the ground and in a hurry to get started somewhere, while maybe its rider was standing with *The Hoosier Schoolmaster* in his hand, looking at the picture of the schoolhouse, and then maybe looking at the ridiculous-looking snowman we'd made of him.

In a few minutes Poetry and I were so out of wind that we had to stop and walk awhile, especially because I had a pain in my right side which I sometimes get when I run too fast too long. "My side hurts," I said to Poetry.

He said, "Better stop and stoop down and unbuckle your boot, and buckle it again, and it'll quit hurting."

"It'll *what?*" I said, thinking his idea was crazy.

42

"It'll quit hurting if you stop and stoop down and unbuckle your boot and then buckle it again."

Well, I couldn't run anymore with the sharp pain in my side, so even though I thought Poetry's idea was crazy, I stopped and stooped over, biting off my mittens with my teeth, and laying them down on the snow for a jiffy and unbuckling one of my boots and buckling it again while I was still stooped over. Then I straightened up, and would you believe it? That crazy ache in my side was actually gone! There wasn't even a sign of it.

I panted a minute longer to get my wind, then we started on the run again. "It's crazy," I said, "but it worked. How come?"

"Poetry Thompson's father told me," he said, puffing along ahead of me, "only it won't work in the summertime. In the summertime you have to stop running, and stop and stoop down and pick up a rock, and spit on it and turn it over and lay it down again very carefully upside down, and your side will quit hurting."

Right then I stumbled over a log and fell down on my face, and scrambled to my feet and we hurried on. I said to Poetry, "What do you do when you get a sore toe from stumping it on a log—stoop over and scrape the snow off the log and kiss it, and turn it over, and then—?"

It wasn't any time to be funny, only worried, but Poetry explained to me that it was the *stooping* that was what did it. "It's getting your body bent double that does it. Hey! Look! There he is now!"

I looked in the direction of our house since we were getting pretty close to Bumblebee hill and, sure enough, there was our teacher sitting on his great big beautiful brown horse which was standing and prancing right beside the old iron pitcher pump not more than twenty feet from our back door. Mom was standing there with her sweater on, talking to him or maybe listening to him. Then I saw Mr. Black tip his hat like an honest-to-goodness gentleman, and bow, and his pretty horse whirled about and went in a horse hurry to our front gate, which was being held open by my dad, and he went galloping up the road. His horse was galloping in the shadow which they both made on the snowy road ahead of them.

Well, that was that, I thought. Poetry and I, who were at the top of Bumblebee hill, hurried down to where we had left our sleds, the rest of the gang having taken theirs with them when we'd gone to the cave. At the bottom of the hill, we saw the great big tall snowman. The sun was still shining right straight on it, but wouldn't be pretty soon because it would go down. So Poetry and I stopped close to it, and he got his camera ready.

"You get *The Hoosier Schoolmaster*, Bill, and turn it around and stand it up against the Hoosier schoolmaster's stomach," Poetry ordered, "so I can get a good picture of it."

I started to do what he said and then gasped. *There wasn't any Hoosier Schoolmaster!* The book was gone. "It's gone!" I said to Poetry, and it was. There was a page of yellow writing paper instead.

"Hey!" I said. "There's something printed on it!" Sure enough, there was. The piece of yellow writing tablet was standing up on the two sticks, leaning against the snowman's stomach, and was fastened so the wind wouldn't blow it away, by another stick stuck through the paper and into the snowman's stomach.

"It's your poem, Poetry," I said, remembering the poem which Poetry had written about our teacher. "How'd it get here?" Right away I was reading the poem again, which was almost funny, only I didn't feel like laughing because of wondering who had stolen the book and had put the poem here in its place. The poem was written exactly right:

The Sugar Creek Gang had the worst of teachers,
*   And "Black" his name was called,*
His round red face had the homeliest of features,
*   He was fat and forty and bald.*

It had been funny the first time I had read it, which was not more than a week ago, but for some reason right that minute it was anything in the world else. I was gritting my teeth and wondering who had done it, and who had stolen *The Hoosier Schoolmaster*. There wasn't one of the gang that *could* have done it, 'cause we had all been together all afternoon; and from the cave all the rest of the gang had gone home.

"Who in the world wrote it and put it there?" I said, noticing that the printing was very large and had been put on with black crayola, the kind we used in school.

"There's only one other person in the world who knows I wrote that poem," Poetry said, "and that's Shorty Long."

"Shorty Long!" I said, remembering the newest boy who had moved into our neighborhood and was almost as fat as Poetry and who had been the cause of most of our trouble with our new teacher and had had two or three fights with me and had licked the stuffin's out of me once, and I had licked the stuffin's out of him once also, even worse than he had me almost.

"How'd he find out?" I asked.

"Dragonfly told him."

I remembered right that minute that Dragonfly and Shorty Long had been kind of chummy last week and we had all worried for fear there was maybe going to be trouble in our own gang which there'd never been before, and all because of the new fat guy who had moved into our neighborhood and had started coming to our school.

"Are you going to take a picture of it?" I asked Poetry.

He said, "I certainly am; I'm going to have the evidence and then I can prove to anybody that doesn't believe it, that somebody actually put it here."

"Yeah," I said, "but everybody knows *you* wrote the poem."

Poetry lowered his camera, and just that minute I saw something else that made me stare and in fact startled me so that for a jiffy I was almost as much excited as I had been when the fierce, mad, old mother bear had been trying to kill Little Jim right at that very place where we were about a year and a half ago.

"Hey! Look!" I said, "Mr. Black's been here himself!"

"Mr. *Black!*" Poetry said in almost a half scream. And right away both of us were looking down in the snow around the beech tree, and around the snowman. Sure enough, there were horse's tracks, the kind of tracks that showed that the horse had shoes on. And even while I was scared and wondering, What on earth! there popped into my red head the crazy superstition that if you found a horseshoe and put it up over the door of your

47

house or one of the rooms of your house, you would have good luck.

"I'll bet Mr. Black took the book and wrote the poem and put it here."

"He wouldn't," I said, but was afraid he might have.

"I'm going to take a picture anyway," Poetry said, and stepped back and took one, and then real quick, took another. Then he took the yellow sheet of paper with the poem on it and folded it up and put it in his coat pocket. And with our faces and minds worried, we started in fiercely knocking the living daylights out of that snowman. The first thing we did was to pull off the red nose, and pull out the corncob pipe, and knock the round head off and watch it go ker-swish onto the ground and break in pieces, then we pulled the sticks out of his stomach, kicked him in the same place, and in a jiffy had him looking like nothing.

We felt pretty mixed up in our minds, I can tell you.

"Do you suppose Mr. Black did that?" I said.

"He wouldn't," Poetry said "But if he rode his horse down here and saw it, he'll certainly think we're a bunch of heathen."

"We aren't though—are we?" I said to Poetry. For some reason I was remembering that Little Jim had acted like maybe we shouldn't make *fun* of our teacher just 'cause he had hair only all around his head and not on top, and couldn't help it. For some reason, it didn't seem very funny right that minute, and it seemed like Little Jim was right.

"What about *The Hoosier Schoolmaster?*" I asked Poetry as we dragged our sleds up Bumblebee hill. "What'll we tell your mother? And what'll she tell Mrs. Mansfield?"

"I don't know," Poetry said, his voice sounding more worried than I'd heard it in a long time.

The first thing Mom said to us when we got to our house was, "Mr. Black was here twice this afternoon."

"Twice?" I said. "What for? What did he want?"

"Oh, he was just visiting around, getting acquainted with the parents of the boys. Such a beautiful brown saddle horse," Mom said. "And he was so polite."

"The horse?" Poetry said.

But Mom ignored his remark and said, "He took a picture of our house and barn and tried to get one of Mixy cat, but Mixy was scared of the horse, I guess, and ran like a frightened rabbit."

"Was he actually taking pictures?" Poetry asked with a worried voice.

"Yes, and he wanted to get one of you boys playing on Bumblebee hill. But you were all gone, he said, but he found the book you left there, so he brought it back—you know, the one Mrs. Mansfield wanted."

"What book?" I said, pretending to be surprised. "Did Mrs. Mansfield want a book?"

And Mom who was standing at our back door bareheaded, and shouldn't have been because she might catch cold, said, "Yes, she phoned here for *The Hoosier Schoolmaster* while Mr. Black was here, but I knew your mother had one, Poetry, so I told her to call there."

Poetry and I were looking at each other, wondering, What on earth?

Then Mom said, "Mr. Black thought maybe you boys had been reading it or something and had forgotten it when you left."

"D-d-did he—did he—?" Poetry began, but stuttered so much he had to stop and start again. "Did he say *where* he found it? I mean was it—that is, where did he *find* it?"

"He didn't say," Mom said. "But he said since he was going over to Mrs. Mansfield's anyway, he'd take it over for me; so you won't have to take it over, Bill," Mom finished.

Well, that was that. Poetry and I sighed to each other, and he said, "Did you tell my mother?"

"I've just called her," Mom said, "and you're to come on home right away to get the chores done early. It's early to bed for all of us on Saturday night, you know."

Poetry must have felt pretty bad, just like I did,

but he managed to say politely to Mom, "Thank you, Mrs. Collins. I'll hurry right home."

I walked out to the gate with him, and for a jiffy we just stood and looked at each other, both of us with worried looks on our faces.

"Do you suppose he really took a picture of himself with that poem on his stomach?" Poetry asked. "And if he did, *who* on earth put it there?"

"I don't know," I said, "but what would he want with pictures of all of us and our parents?"

"I'm sure I don't know," Poetry said, with a worried voice.

Just that minute Pop called from the barn and said, "Bill, hurry up and gather the eggs! It'll be too dark to see in the barn as soon as the sun goes down! Poetry, be sure to come again sometime," which was Dad's way of telling Poetry to step on the gas and get going home right now, which Poetry did. I went back to the house and got the egg basket to start to gather eggs, wondering what would happen next.

6

J UST AS I STARTED to open our kitchen door and go out to the barn, Mom came from the other room where she'd been talking on the phone and said, "Little Jim's mother is coming down with the flu and won't be able to go to church tomorrow, so we're to pick up Little Jim and also stop for Tom Till and take him to church with us. We'll have to get up a little earlier tomorrow morning, so you get the chores done quick so we can get supper over and go to bed nice and early." I thought that was a good idea. I was already tired all of a sudden, almost too tired to gather eggs.

Tomorrow, though, would be a fine day. It'd be fun to stop at Little Jim's and Tom Till's houses and to take them to church with us.

Little Jim had something on his mind that was bothering him though, and I wondered what it was. Also, I wondered who was coming to our house for dinner tomorrow. Maybe it would be Little Jim, as *well* as somebody else, if his mom was going to have the flu.

Pretty soon I was up in our haymow all by my-self carrying the egg basket around to the different places where different ones of our old hens laid their eggs. Old Bent-comb still laid her daily egg up in a corner of the mow so I climbed over a big stack of sweet-smelling hay to where I knew the nest was. I wasn't feeling very good inside because things hadn't gone right during the day, and yet I couldn't tell what was wrong, except maybe it was just me. When I got to old Bent-comb's nest, sure enough there were two eggs in it—one was the pretty white egg Bent-comb herself had laid that day and the other was an artificial glass egg which we kept in the nest all the time just to encourage any hen that might see it, to stop and lay an egg there herself, just as if maybe there had been another hen who had thought it was a good place to lay an egg. It was easy to fool old Bent-comb, I thought.

While I was getting ready to go back to the lad-der and go down it to the main floor of the barn, my eyes climbed up Dad's brand new ladder which goes up to the cupola at the very peak of the roof of our very high barn. It certainly was a very nice light ladder, and next summer it would be easy for me to carry it to one cherry tree after another in our orchard when I helped pick cherries for Mom. It was such a light ladder, even Little Jim could carry it. While I was standing looking up and think-ing about wishing spring would hurry up and come,

I all of a sudden wanted to climb up the ladder and look out the windows of the cupola and see what I could see in the different directions around the Sugar Creek territory. Also, I wondered if Snow-white, my favorite pigeon, and her husband had decided to have their nest in the cupola again this year, and if there were maybe any eggs or maybe a couple of baby pigeons, although parent pigeons hardly ever decided to raise any baby pigeons in the wintertime. If there was anything I liked to look at more than anything else, it was baby birds in a nest. Their fuzz always reminded me of Big Jim's fuzzy moustache, he being the only one of the Sugar Creek Gang to begin to have any.

In a jiffy I was on my way and in another jiffy I was there, standing on the second from the top rung of the ladder. It was nice and light up there with the sun still shining in, although pretty soon it would go down. In one direction I could see Poetry's house, and their big maple tree right close beside it in the backyard, under which in the summertime he always pitched his tent and sometimes he would invite me to stay all night with him. In another direction, and far away across our cornfield, was Dragonfly's house which had an orchard close by it, where in the fall of the year we could all have all the apples we wanted. Big Jim and Circus lived right across the road from each other, but I couldn't see either one of their houses, or Little Tom's because Little Tom

54

lived across the bridge on the other side of Sugar Creek. I could see our red-brick schoolhouse, away on past Dragonfly's house though. But when I looked at it, instead of feeling kind of happy inside like I nearly always did when we had our pretty woman teacher for a teacher, I felt kind of sad.

There was the big maple tree which I knew was right close beside a tall iron pump, near which we had built a snow fort. Behind that was the wood-shed where we'd been locked in by our new man teacher, and behind the woodshed was the great big school yard where we played baseball and blind-man's buff and other games in the fall and spring, and where we play fox and geese in the winter. For a few minutes I forgot I was supposed to be gathering eggs, and was doing what Dad is always accusing me of doing, which is dreaming. I was thinking about what had happened that afternoon, such as the trip we'd taken through the cave to Old Man Paddler's cabin, and the prayer he'd said for all of us, and especially for old hook-nosed John Till, which Little Tom had heard, and it had made him cry and want to go home. Poor Little Tom, I thought. What if I had had a dad like his, instead of the kind of wonderful dad I had, who made it easy for Mom to be happy, which is why maybe Mom was always singing around our kitchen, even when she was tired, and also why, whenever Dad came into our house after being gone awhile,

55

Mom would look up quick from whatever she was doing and give him a nice look, and sometimes they'd be awful glad to see each other, and Dad would give her a great big hug like dads are supposed to do to moms. Poor Little Tom's mom, I thought.

Well, while I was still not thinking about finishing gathering the eggs, I looked in the last direction I hadn't looked yet. That was toward our house and over the top of the spreading branches of the plum tree and over the top of our gate which Dragonfly had had his ride on, and on down toward Bumblebee hill where we'd coasted and had fun and made the snowman of Mr. Black. Say! Right that second I saw something moving—in fact, it was somebody's cap moving along just below the crest of the hill, but all I could see was the bobbing-up-and-down cap, and right away I knew whose cap it was—it was the bright red cap of the new tough guy in our neighborhood whose name was Shorty Long. And right away I knew who it was that had written Poetry's poetry and put it on the sticks into Mr. Black's stomach.

I had a queer and also an angry feeling inside me 'cause I just *knew* Mr. Black had seen the poem and, since it had been signed "The Sugar Creek Gang," we would all be in for still more trouble Monday morning in school.

While I was standing up there in that cupola, I

made up my mind that no matter how much we didn't like our teacher, and no matter what ideas Poetry and I had once had in our minds to find out whether a board on the top of the schoolhouse chimney would smoke out a teacher, I, Bill Collins wasn't going to vote yes if the gang put it to a vote to decide whether to do it or not. No sir, not me.

Right that second, I heard my dad calling me from down on the main floor of the barn. "Better come on down and finish your chores, Bill." I started to climb backward down the new ladder very carefully to the haymow floor and then down the other ladder to the main floor of the barn.

Dad had just finished milking our one milk cow, and the big three-gallon milk pail was full clear to the top and there was inch-high, creamy-yellow foam above the top of the pail. Mixy, our old black and white cat, was mewing and mewing and walking all around Dad's legs and looking up and mewing and rubbing her sides against his boots and also running over toward the little milk pan over by a corner of the barn floor, as if to say to Dad, "For goodness sake, I may be a mere cat, but does that give you any right to make me wait for my supper?"

Anyway I was reminded that I was hungry myself, and pretty soon we'd all be in our house, sitting around our table and eating raw-fried potatoes and reddish slices of fried ham, and other things—

57

ll take the milk to the house, Bill," Dad said. "You follow me up to the back porch, Mixy—you can have fresh milk tonight—and also, only a little raw meat, because there are absolutely too many mice around this barn. Any ordinary hungry cat ought to catch at least one mouse a day, Mixy, and if you don't catch them, we'll have to make you hungry, so you will. Understand?" I looked at Dad's big reddish-blackish eyebrows and he was frowning at Mixy, although I knew he liked her a lot, but didn't like mice very well.

I finished gathering the eggs that were in the barn and then went to the hen house where I knew there would be some more eggs, and then took my basket of maybe four dozen eggs toward the house.

Mixy was there on the back porch, I noticed, lapping away at her milk like a house afire. I wiped off my boots carefully like I'd been trained to do whether I was at home or in somebody else's house, pushed open the door to our kitchen and went in, expecting to see Mom or Dad, or both of them there. But there wasn't anybody there, so I set the egg basket down on Mom's worktable, and started into the front room, where I thought they'd be. All of a sudden I heard Mom saying something in a tearful voice, and I stopped cold—wondering what I'd maybe done and shouldn't have, and if Mom was telling Dad about it. So I started to listen, and then was half afraid to, so I started to open the door

58

and go out when I heard Dad say in a low voice, "No, Mother, whatever it is, I know one thing—our Bill will tell the truth. He'd tell the truth right now if I asked him, but I'm not going to. I'm going to wait and see what happens, and see if he'll tell me himself."

I strained my ears hard to hear what Mom would answer. She said, "All right, Theodore, I'll be patient; but just the same, I'm worried."

"Don't you worry one little tiny bit, Mother," Dad said. "A boy's heart is like a garden. If you plant good seed in it, and cultivate and plow it and water it with love, he'll come out all right." That made me like my dad a lot.

Only I didn't have time to think about it 'cause right that very second almost, I heard Mom say in a worried voice, "Yes, dear, but *weeds* grow in a garden without anyone planting them." This made me feel all sad inside, and for some reason I could see our own garden which every spring and summer had all kinds of weeds—ragweeds, smartweeds, and big ugly jimsonweeds, and lots of other kinds.

Right that second, I remembered something my dad had said to me once last summer which was, "Say, Bill, do you know how to keep the big weeds out of our garden, without having to pull up or cut out even one of them?" And when I said, "No, how, Dad?" he said, "Just kill all of them while they are *little*."

Well, I didn't want Mom or Dad to know I'd heard them talking about me, so I sneaked out the back door very carefully and started talking in a friendly voice to Mixy, saying to her, "Listen, Mixy, do you know how to keep all the great big mice out of our barn? You just catch all the mice while they're little—it's as easy as pie."

Mixy looked up from her empty milk pan and mewed and looked down at her pan again, and looked up at me again and mewed again, and then walked over to me and rubbed her sides against my boots like she liked me a lot. For some reason, I thought Mixy was a very nice cat right that minute, so I said to her, "I'm awful glad you like me, Mixy, even if nobody else around this place does."

Pretty soon Dad and I were out doing the rest of the chores while Mom was getting supper. Almost right away it began to get dark, and we went in to supper. "Wash your hands and go get Charlotte Ann," Mom said to me. "I think she's awake now."

Charlotte Ann is my baby sister and, even though she is a girl, is a pretty swell baby; in fact, she's wonderful.

In a few minutes Dad and Mom and Charlotte Ann and I were all sitting around our kitchen table in the lamplight. We had two kerosene lamps lit, one of them behind me on the high shelf above my head, and the other on another shelf above the water pail in the corner.

60

We always bowed our heads at our house before every meal, different ones of us asking the blessing, whichever one of us Dad called on. When I was little I said a little poem prayer, but didn't do it anymore because Dad thought I was too big. Since I was an actual Christian, in spite of having jimson-weeds in my heart, I always prayed whenever Dad told me to, only I hoped that he wouldn't ask me to tonight. Dad looked around the table at all of us, and Mom helped Charlotte Ann fold her hands, which she didn't want to do, but kept wiggling and squirming and reaching for things on the table, which were too far away. "Well, let's see—whom shall we ask to pray tonight?" Dad said.

His question was cut short by the telephone ringing our ring, which meant that one of us had to answer the phone. "I'll get it," I said, "maybe it's one of the gang—"

"I'll get it," Mom said, "I'm expecting a call—I say, *I'll get it!*" Mom raised her voice because I was already out of my chair and halfway to the living room door.

When Mom came back a minute later, she was smiling like she'd had some wonderful news. She said, "It was Mrs. Long. Mr. Long won't be home tomorrow, so she can go to church with us. Isn't that wonderful? It's an answer to prayer."

I spoke up then and said, "How about Shorty? Is he going too?"

I don't know what there was in my voice that shouldn't have been when I asked that question, but Mom said in an astonished tone of voice, "Why, Bill Collins! The very idea! Don't you *want* him to go to church and Sunday school and learn something about being a Christian? Do you want him to grow up to be a heathen? What's the matter with you?"

I gulped. Mom had read my thoughts like an open book. "Of course," I said, "he ought to go to church, but—"

"But *what?*" Mom said.

"He's awful mean to the gang," I said, "He—"

"Perhaps we'd better ask the blessing now," Dad said in a kind voice, and right away we bowed our heads while Dad prayed a short prayer, which ended something like this: ". . . and bless our minister tomorrow. Put into his heart the things he ought to say that will do us all the most good . . . . Make his sermon like a plow and hoe and rake that will make the gardens of our hearts what they all ought to be . . . . Bless Shorty Long and his mother and father, and the Till family, all of which we ask in Jesus' name. Amen."

For some reason when Dad finished, I seemed to feel like maybe I didn't actually *hate* our new teacher, not very much anyway, and I thought maybe Shorty Long, even if he was a terribly tough boy, would be better if he had somebody pull some of the weeds out of him.

After supper, we all took our regular Saturday night baths and went to bed. The next thing we knew it was a wonderful morning, with the sun shining on the snow and with sleigh bells jingling on people's horses because some of our neighbors lived on roads where the snowplow hadn't been through yet, and couldn't use their cars and so had to use sleds instead. It was going to be a wonderful day all day, I thought, and was glad I was alive.

7

Just before nine o'clock we all started in our car toward Little Jim's house, which was closer than Tom Till's or Shorty Long's. Little Jim came tumbling out his back door, his short legs carrying him fast out to the road. He got in and I was certainly tickled to see him. Mom and Dad and Charlotte Ann were in the front seat so Charlotte Ann would be closer to our car heater and keep warm because it was a cold morning.

"How is your mother this morning?" Mom asked Little Jim.

Little Jim piped up in his mouselike voice, "She's better than last night. Dad and I took breakfast to her in bed." That is what *my* dad does to *my* mom when she doesn't feel well. In fact, sometimes when Dad gets up extra early before Mom does, he sneaks out into our kitchen quietly and makes coffee and carries a cupful in and surprises Mom even when she is perfectly well, which Dad says is maybe one reason why Mom keeps on liking him so well.

Our car turned north on the road that leads to Tom's house, crossed the snow-covered Sugar Creek bridge, and went on. While we were on the bridge, Little Jim said to me, "Look, there's an oak tree that still has its leaves on, and'll maybe keep 'em on all winter."

Then we came to Tom's weathered, old-looking house and barn, and Dad pulled up at the side of the road in front of their mailbox which had "John Till" on it, and honked the horn for Tom to come out and get in.

There was a new path which maybe Tom had scooped for his mom so she could get the mail. In a minute now, I thought, their side door would open and Little Tom would come zipping out, with his kind of old-looking coat on and he would come crunch, crunch, crunch through the snow path to where we were. Tom didn't come right away though. Dad honked again so Tom would be sure to hear. Then when he still didn't come and there wasn't any curtain moving at their window to let us know anybody was home and that Tom would be here in a minute, Mom said to me, "Bill, you better run in and tell him we're here. We have to stop at Longs' yet, and we don't want to be late."

Almost in a second I was opening the door and getting out. Little Jim tumbled out right after me, saying, "I'll go with you," and since neither his mom nor his dad were there to tell him not to, both of us went squishing up the snow path toward their side door. There had been a little wind during the night, and some snow had drifted into the path, and I was glad we had on our boots, so our good Sunday shoes wouldn't get wet and spoil their shine.

I knocked at Tom's door and waited, but nobody answered. Little Jim and I listened to see what we could hear, but all I could hear was somebody moving around inside like he was in a hurry—like maybe there had been some things on the floor and he was in a hurry to straighten up the room or the house because company was coming.

Then I heard a door shutting somewhere in the house, and I knew it was the door between their living room and kitchen. Then I heard footsteps coming toward our door, and I wondered what was wrong. I was sure something was but didn't know what.

The next thing I knew the door opened in front of me and there stood little red-haired Tom, with his hair mussed up, and his old clothes on, and his eyes were kind of red and it looked like he had been crying. "I'm sorry," he said, "but I can't go. Mother's got the flu, and I have to take care of her and keep the fires going."

"Can't your daddy do that?" Little Jim asked in a disappointed voice.

Little Tom swallowed hard like there was a tear in his throat and said, "Daddy's not home again. He—he's—not home."

I knew what he meant, but he was ashamed to

say it. It probably was that his dad had gotten drunk again and was maybe right that very minute in the Sugar Creek jail.

"Where's Bob?" Little Jim wanted to know.

Tom stood there in the half-open kitchen door and said, "He got up early and went over to Shorty Long's; they're going to hunt pigeons."

I knew what that meant 'cause sometimes some of the farmers in our neighborhood had too many pigeons, and the Sugar Creek Gang would go to their different barns and shut all the doors and windows quick and help catch the pigeons for them, and you could get sometimes fifteen cents apiece for them if you sold them.

If Shorty Long and Bob had gone hunting pigeons together, it meant that Shorty Long wouldn't want to go to Sunday school with us when we stopped at their house after a while to get his mother to take her to church with us. It also meant that Shorty and Bob had maybe decided to like each other since neither one of them liked the Sugar Creek Gang.

Little Tom didn't know what I'd been thinking, so he piped up and said to Little Jim, "I'm sorry I can't go, but I can't. You tell Teacher I'll try to come next week, and tell her I studied my Sunday school lesson, and—wait a minute!" Tom turned and, leaving the door open, hurried back inside the house, opened the door to their living room and went in, like he had gone after something. He shut the door after him real quick, like he was trying to keep the cold air in the kitchen from getting into that other room.

In that split minute while the door was open though, I saw that they had a big double bed in their living room and that Tom's mother was in it, all covered up. There was a small table beside her bed with a glass half full of water, but the room looked kind of topsy-turvy like the housekeeping was being done by a boy instead of a mother.

A second later Tom was out again, shutting the door behind him, and coming right straight to Little Jim and me, and holding out his hand and saying, "Here—here's my offering." He handed me a small offering envelope like the ones we used in our church, and without trying to, I noticed it had two very small coins in it, and I guessed they were dimes, which maybe Tom himself had saved from catching pigeons.

Just that second, Tom's mother coughed, a kind of sad, sick cough that sounded like maybe she was a lot sicker than she ought to be. I knew that if my mom was as sick as that Dad would have a doctor out to see her right away, so I said, "Has the doctor been here?"

Little Tom frowned and said, "Nope, we can't— nope, I guess Mom will get well. She always does."

Just that second our car honked, and I knew

the folks were wondering what on earth was keeping us so long. There didn't seem to be anything we could do, but I knew somebody ought to do something for Tom's mom, 'cause that cough sounded dangerous. *Why she might even get pneumonia,* I thought; *she might even have it now.*

As quick as Little Jim and I reached the car, and had climbed into the back seat, we told Mom and Dad. While I was excitedly telling them, I noticed that the muscles in Dad's jaws were working and I knew he was thinking, and also was half angry inside because anybody had to have such a mean husband as old hook-nosed John Till.

"He's a slave," Dad said, thinking of Tom's dad.

Mom said, with a very determined voice, "Theodore, you take the boys on to Sunday school. Be sure to stop for Mrs. Long. Here, Bill, you hold Charlotte Ann. If Mrs. Till has the flu, I can't keep Charlotte Ann here with me."

Dad started to say something, but Mom had already made up her mind, and it was too late. Mom was already halfway out of the car when she said, "You can come on back and get me in time for church—no, wait a minute. I want Tom to go to Sunday school too—I'll send him right out."

Mom was out of the car and going up the snow path toward the old house when Little Jim piped up and said, "The doctor's going to stop at our house at ten o'clock to see Mother. I'll bet he'd stop to see Tom's mother too if anybody asked him to."

"They can't afford a doctor," I said, remembering what Tom had tried to say a few minutes ago.

But I hadn't any more than got the words out of my mouth than Dad spoke up almost fiercely, like he was angry at somebody or something, and this is what he said: "But *I* can. If Tom's mother needs a doctor, she's going to have one." With that Dad shoved open the car door at his left side, saying, "You boys wait here a minute. I'll be right back." He slammed the door and circled the car and went swishing with very determined steps through that snow path to Tom's side door, and disappeared inside, leaving Little Jim and Charlotte Ann and me in the car. The motor was running and the heater fan was circulating warm air all over the car, so we wouldn't get cold.

I still had Little Tom's offering envelope in my hand, and it reminded me of how maybe Tom had earned the money. So I said to Little Jim, "I hope Shorty Long and Bob don't stop at our barn 'cause we don't have too many pigeons. And besides, there's a nest up in our cupola with some baby pigeons in it, and if they catch the mother and father the babies will freeze or maybe starve to death."

A jiffy later, Dad came out to the car, bringing

Tom with him, and all of us except Mom drove on toward Shorty Long's house to get Shorty's mother.

Pretty soon, fifteen minutes later maybe, we all pulled up in our car in front of the little white church on top of the hill right across from a two-room brick schoolhouse where the Sugar Creek Literary Society met once a month on Wednesday nights. All of us except Dad got out to go inside the church. Shorty Long's mother was carrying Charotte Ann and was going to take care of her until Dad got back.

"I'm going to the parsonage to call the doctor to stop at your house," Dad said to Tom, "and I'm taking a radio to your mother, so if she feels able she can listen to a gospel program."

I looked quick at Little Tom, knowing he might feel ashamed to be reminded that his folks couldn't afford a doctor, and also that they didn't have a radio, and knowing it was because of his dad. But Tom was looking in another direction and was swallowing hard like he had taken too big a bite of something and hadn't chewed it long enough but was trying to swallow it. Then he whirled around real quick and hurried up the cement steps to the church's door, with Little Jim and me right after him.

Just inside the vestibule, fastened to the wall, was what is called "The Minister's Question Box," with a little slit in the top for people to put in Bible questions they wanted explained, or also for any extra offering people wanted the minister to have. Right that second I saw Little Jim pull one of his small hands out of his pocket and slip a folded piece of paper into the box, kind of bashful like, then all of us went to where our classes would be sitting.

As soon as Sunday school was over and church started, I noticed Mr. Black come in. I was surprised to see him come to church, but I knew our minister would preach a good sermon like he always does, and it wouldn't hurt even a schoolteacher to hear a good sermon maybe once a week.

8

TWO OR THREE TIMES while our minister was preaching a very interesting sermon which a boy could understand, my thoughts flew away like they were birds with wings, and for quite a while I didn't even know I was in church because I was far away in my thoughts. As you may know, our minister was Sylvia's father, and Sylvia was a very polite, kind of pretty girl with a good singing voice. She always had her hair looking very neat and pretty with a ribbon or something in it like girls wear in their hair, and she was Big Jim's favorite girl. I was sitting beside Big Jim, and Dragonfly was beside me, with the rest of the Sugar Creek Gang in different places in the church. Our parents didn't let us all sit together if they could help it because the minister got more attention himself if we sat in different places—not that any of us tried to be mischievous in church—in fact, we always had to try not to be.

Right that second Sylvia's kind-voiced dad was talking about how wonderful it was when you knew you had done something wrong, and were sorry for it that you could pray right straight to the Lord Himself and confess your sins right straight to Him, and He would make your heart clean. "The blood of Jesus Christ, the Son of God, will cleanse you from all sin, *right that very minute*," Sylvia's dad said. It seemed like a wonderful thing to believe, and made me feel good all inside of me.

And then almost right away, he went on to say, quoting another verse from the Bible, "Come now, let us reason together, saith the LORD: though your sins be as scarlet, they shall be as white as snow; though they be red like crimson, they shall be as wool." I had learned that verse by heart once in a summer Bible school. And all of a sudden, my thoughts were flying away, and I was remembering Poetry's pet lamb whose wool was *not* white one morning when the lamb fell down in a mud puddle, and I was remembering Poetry's funny poetry:

> *Poetry had a little lamb,*
> *Its fleece a dirty black,*
> *The only place its wool was white*
> *Was high up on its back.*

Also I was at that very minute reminded of another poem which I had seen yesterday, which was written on yellow paper and which had been pinned with a brown stick on the white stomach of a snowman. That poem still didn't seem funny, and for some reason I decided I was going to try

74

to be what is called a gentleman, and try to act like one in school, even if I didn't like my teacher.

I didn't hear any more of Sylvia's dad's sermon for a while because I happened to look out the church window, which didn't have stained glass like some of the churches in town did, and I saw somebody's barn just on the other side of the little cemetery. There were a lot of pigeons flying around over the barn, and in the sky. Right away I was remembering Shorty Long and Big Bob Till, and wondering where they were and what they were doing.

I had a heavy feeling inside of me that they would maybe visit all of the barns of the Sugar Creek Gang's dads and catch a lot of pigeons, and maybe they'd catch and kill the pretty brown and white pair of pigeons which had their nest in the cupola of our barn, and then what would happen to the *baby* pigeons?

Dad didn't come to church at all because of deciding to stay with Mom, but he was there in the car right afterward. All of us, including Little Jim and Tom Till and Mrs. Long and Charlotte Ann, shook hands with a lot of people and climbed into our car and drove away. Dad and all of us were talking and listening as our car went purring down the road. We were just stopping at Shorty Long's house to let Mrs. Long out when Little Jim said to me in a half whisper, "Sylvia's dad certainly preached a good sermon. I *thought* that was why some houses didn't have as much snow on their roofs as others, and why barns always have more snow than houses that people live in. It was a good sermon."

"What?" I said to Little Jim, not remembering anything in the sermon about snow on people's houses or barns. Sylvia's dad must have said that when I was thinking about snowy white wool on Poetry's lamb—or else about a snowman standing at the bottom of Bumblebee hill.

Pretty soon we came to Tom Till's house. Dad had already told us the doctor had been there, and Mrs. Till didn't have pneumonia, only a bad chest cold.

Dad had gone to our house to get one of our radios so Mrs. Till could hear a good Christian program, and she was feeling a lot better. Dad also had told us that Bob had come home while Mom was taking care of Mrs. Till, but he had gone away again. "Did he have any pigeons?" little red-haired Tom asked when Dad started to get out and go in with Tom and get Mom.

"About a dozen," Dad told him. "He put them in the pigeon cage out in the woodshed."

Right away I spoke up and said, "Were there any *white* ones?" remembering the beautiful white pigeon with pink eyes which had her nest up in the cupola of our barn, and whose big beautiful brown husband was so proud of her and always was cooing to her when they were on the roof of our barn and was always strutting around so very proud, with his neck all puffed out like he was very important.

"I don't know," Dad said.

I said, "Can I go and look, Tom?"

Tom said, "Sure, I'll go with you."

"Let me hold Charlotte Ann," Little Jim said, because he liked to hold babies on his small lap anyway.

Dad went in to get Mom, and Tom and I went into their woodshed to look through the wire cage at about fifteen very pretty pigeons.

All of a sudden while I was looking, I got a hot feeling all inside of me 'cause right there in front of my eyes with the other different-colored pigeons, was a beautiful albino one—the prettiest snow-white one I ever saw with pretty pink eyes, and I knew right away it was my favorite pigeon, old Snow-white herself, who had her nest in the cupola of our barn.

"There's my pigeon!" I cried to Little Tom.

When he asked me which one and I told him, he said, "Are you sure?"

"I'm positive," I said. "See that little brown spot just below the left pink eye. I'm going to get her out and take her home."

Little Tom looked and swallowed and got a

very scared expression on his face and started to say something, and then stopped.

"'Smatter?" I said.

He said, "Nothing, only—"

"Only what?" I asked him.

"Only—only Bob's got a terrible temper, and he's already mad at me."

Say, when I saw the scared expression on that little guy's face, I realized that if I let Snow-white out of that cage, Tom would maybe get a terrible beating from his big brother, and it'd be my fault. Just that minute, Dad and Mom came out of the side door of Tom's house, and it was time for us to go home. Mom was going to hurry with our own dinner, which had nearly all been cooked yesterday, and we were going to bring some nice chicken soup back in the car for Tom's mom's dinner, and also some chicken for Tom himself.

I still didn't know who was coming to our house for dinner, and whoever did come would have to wait awhile because Mom would have to finish preparing it. "Who's coming to our house for dinner?" I asked.

Mom said, as we all started down the road toward Little Jim's house, "A certain very fine gentleman named Little Jim Foote of the Sugar Creek Gang." Was I ever glad! But as the car glided down the white road, I kept thinking of my pretty Snow-white in Bob Till's cage, and I knew that

78

Bob would maybe kill her along with all the other pigeons and sell them at the Sugar Creek poultry shop.

Just that second, just as we were getting close to Little Jim's house, Little Jim said, "Hey, Bill! Look! There goes a white pigeon, flying all by itself."

I looked out the car window and sure enough, there was a snow-white pigeon with its white wings flapping, and it was diving along through the Sugar Creek sky right past our car and straight for Sugar Creek and in the direction of our house on the other side of the woods. All of a sudden I got a choked up feeling in my throat 'cause I just *knew* that was my very own Snow-white, and that Tom Till liked me so well he was going to run the risk of getting a terrible beating by his brother Bob by opening their pigeon cage and letting Snow-white out so she could fly home.

For some reason all of a sudden I liked little red-haired Tom Till so well that I wished I could do something very wonderful for him and his sick mother. I just kept my eyes strained on the sky above Sugar Creek and the woods where I'd seen Snow-white disappear, when I heard Little Jim say to me beside me, "Nearly all the snow's melted off our house now."

I looked where he was looking, and he looked

at me, and said, "'Smatter, Bill? You got tears in your eyes."

"Have I?" I said. "I didn't know it."

Tom Till really was a great little guy, I thought, one of my very best friends; and I remembered that before he had started coming to our Sunday school and had become a Christian, he had been one of the meanest boys I ever saw.

I shook my head to knock the tears out of my eyes like Little Jim does when for some reason or other he gets tears in his and doesn't want anybody to know it. Instead of using his handkerchief to wipe them out, he just gives his head a quick jerk or two and, if you happen to be looking at him, you can see the tears fly off in some direction or other.

"Well, here we are!" Dad said, stopping at Little Jim's house for a minute. "You'll probably want your sled. You and Bill will want to coast on Bumblebee hill after dinner." And we did after dinner.

One of the first things we did though, even before we ate dinner, was to go upstairs to my room and both of us put on some old clothes to play in, Little Jim's mother having made him take some old clothes with him when we'd stopped at their house a little while ago.

Right away we were downstairs again, and were on the way through the kitchen to the back door to dash out to the barn to see if Bob Till and Shorty

Long had been there for sure, and also to see if Snow-white had come back and was on her nest up in the cupola, and also find out if her babies were cold or had frozen or something because they didn't have enough feathers on them to keep them warm.

Mom stopped me at the door though, saying, "Bill, if you like, you may wash your hands and finish setting the table—put the bread on, and pour a glass of water for everyone, and milk for you and Jim."

I was surprised at Mom calling Little Jim just Jim, but I sort of felt it was because she thought it made Little Jim sound bigger than he was, and Mom knew it would make him feel good, Mom being a very smart person and knowing how to make boys like her.

"Anything I can do?" Little Jim asked Mom politely. Mom let him pour the water into the glasses for me. When we finished helping her, she said we could go out to the barn if we wanted to, but to be ready to come running as soon as she called us, which we probably would because the oven was open right that minute and I could smell the baked chicken and knew that it was going to be a wonderful dinner.

* * *

"Hi, Mixy!" Little Jim said to our black and white cat which was lying in a cozy nest of her own at the bottom of the ladder which went up to our haymow. Little Jim stooped down to pet her, and she lifted her head without standing up and rubbed the sides of her pretty black and white face against his small hand, and mewed lazily, with half-closed blinking eyes.

I could hardly wait till we got up in the haymow and could climb up Dad's new ladder to the cupola to see if Snow-white was home again, so I started to go up the first ladder, noticing that there was dirt on the ladder that might have been made by somebody with boots or shoes on that had dirty snow on them, and I knew Bob Till and Shorty Long had been there. How many pigeons had they caught? I wondered, and felt an angry feeling inside of me 'cause if there was anything the boys of the Sugar Creek Gang *didn't* do, it was we didn't go into anybody's barn and catch pigeons without the farmer asking us to, or without us first asking the farmer if we could.

Right that minute, while Little Jim was stroking Mixy, and I had my hand and one foot on the ladder ready to start up, I heard Dad's voice calling from somewhere up in the haymow, "Bill! Are you down there?"

"Yeah," I yelled back up to him, "Little Jim and I are *both* here. We're coming up!" Dad's voice had a worried sound in it, and also sounded like maybe I had done something I shouldn't have, or else had maybe left something undone which I should have done.

Then Dad called down to us, and this time it sounded even more like I thought it had, when he said, "Where'd you put my new ladder? I can't find it anywhere."

New ladder! I thought, and wondered, *What on earth!* Why, just yesterday I'd used it to climb up to Snow-white's nest and had left it right there, with the top of it resting on the beam on the south side of the cupola.

"It's right there!" I yelled up to Dad. "Right there in the center of the haymow, going up into the cupola."

"It is not!" Dad yelled back down to me. "And I've looked all over the haymow for it."

I looked at Little Jim, and he was still stooped over stroking Mixy who was standing up now and stretching herself and reaching up with her front claws and doing some kind of monkey business with Little Jim's trousers, taking hold and letting go, and taking hold and letting go, and acting very contented.

Then I went lickety-sizzle up the ladder to the haymow and sure enough Dad was right! The pretty new ladder which he had bought and which I'd left right where I'd told him I'd left it, was gone.

"I left it right here," I said to Dad, and then I had a queer feeling inside of me as I thought about two boys and wondered if they had stolen it. There wasn't a sign of the ladder anywhere in the whole haymow, and I was looking in every direction.

"'Smatter?" Little Jim asked, when his head appeared at the top of the ladder beside where I was standing, and he looked up at my and Dad's astonished faces.

"Somebody's stolen our ladder," I said, "a brand new one Dad just bought last week."

"*Stolen* it?" Little Jim asked, and he had a puzzled expression on his face, and I knew what he was going to say before he said, "Are you sure?" You know, Little Jim always had a hard time believing anybody was bad, or would do anything wrong because he hardly ever did anything wrong himself and, also, 'cause he liked everybody.

Dad said, "No, we're not sure till Bill has tried first to remember if maybe he moved it somewhere else."

I looked all around in a quick circle at the haymow, and I thought that if Bob Till and Shorty Long *had* been there, they might have hidden it under some hay just for meanness. So I got a pitchfork and started to jab it into the hay all around in different places in the haymow. Dad looked in a tunnel under a long beam, and we all looked downstairs and all around. Once I looked up into the cupola and had a half-glad feeling in my heart when I saw Snow-white's white head peeking out over the edge of the beam she had her nest on, like she had just come back and was wondering what on earth anybody wanted with a ladder anyway, she not needing any herself.

Just then we heard Mom calling for dinner and we had to go, all of us being very hungry. I knew Dad was having a hard time believing that I hadn't moved the ladder because many times Dad missed something around the farm and later he or I or somebody had found it where I'd been using it or playing with it, in some place I'd forgotten all about.

But there wasn't any use to look for it. It was gone, and not a one of us knew where—only I was absolutely sure that Bob Till and Shorty Long had hidden it somewhere. I told Mom and Dad what I thought had happened, and we all talked it over pretty excitedly at the dinner table.

After dinner we all looked again, looking all around the barn, inside and out, and also jabbing forks and shovels in the biggest piles of snow around the barn, to see if maybe it had been covered up with snow, and still we couldn't find it. Dad was pretty mad too because about six of our pigeons were missing, and it looked like there had been somebody jumping and running all over the alfalfa hay which we fed to our cows. "How would *you* like to eat a piece of *pie* that some boy's dirty boots had walked all over?" Dad asked. That tickled Little Jim, and he giggled.

Pretty soon Mom and Dad said Little Jim and I could go over to Poetry's house if we wanted to, and we could play in Poetry's nice new basement.

It was while we were at Poetry's house that we saw the ladder, and you'd never in the world guess where it was, and most certainly you'd never in the world guess all the excitement we were going to get mixed up in before the afternoon was over.

9

W E'D BEEN HAVING a wonderful time playing ping pong and checkers, and Little Jim was playing the organ in Poetry's basement while Poetry and I made a lot of noise playing a tie-off game of ping pong, when we heard a door open at the head of the stairway leading down into the basement. Somebody sneezed, and we knew it was Dragonfly who had come over to play with Poetry. Poetry's parents had gone visiting somewhere, calling on some sick people in the Sugar Creek hospital, so we could make more noise and it wouldn't disturb any grownup people's nerves, and would also be good for ours, it being almost as hard on a boy's nerves to be quiet as it is on a grownup person's nerves when a boy is noisy.

Poetry and I stopped our game and yelled up to Dragonfly to come on down and "play the winner," which meant either Poetry or me.

Dragonfly sneezed twice on his way down, he maybe being allergic to something he'd smelled when he came in, or else it was the change from the cold outside air to the warm inside air.

Poetry won that last game, and it meant he was

the champion, so he and Dragonfly started in like a house afire batting that ping pong ball back and forth, back and forth, bang, sock, whiz, sizzle, ping-ping-ping-ping, pong-pong-pong-pong, sock, sock, sock. Say, that little spindle-legged Dragonfly was *good*. He won the first game right off the bat. He really was a good athlete for such a thin little guy. "Hey, you guys!" he said, pretending to be very proud of himself. "Isn't there a window somewhere we can open? I want to throw out my chest." That was an old joke, but it sounded funny for Dragonfly to·say it, his chest being very flat.

"Sure," Poetry said, "but we can get air quicker by opening the door at the top of the stairs," and with that he shuffled up the stairs and opened the door.

Just as he did so, I heard a horse sneeze and a man's voice saying, "Whoa, there, Prince! Stand still!" and I knew it was our new teacher, Mr. Black.

Just that second, Dragonfly sneezed again, and said to Poetry, "I'm allergic to horses. Shut that door!"

"Hello!" a voice called. "Anybody at home?"

Well, I can't tell you all that happened for the next fifteen minutes because I have to hurry with the rest of this story, but Mr. Black was very kind to us boys. He came down into the basement and took a flashbulb picture of us with our ping pong balls and paddles and with Little Jim at the organ, and didn't say a word about the snowman we knew he'd seen yesterday, or the book, or anything. He was very nice, and a little later when he rode away on his great big beautiful prancing saddle horse, I thought maybe he was going to be a good teacher after all. The last thing he said to us just before he swung prancing Prince around and jogged up Poetry's lane was, "Well, I'll see you boys in the morning at school. I'm going to ride over now and get the fire started. I let it go out over Saturday to save fuel. But the weather report is for a cold wave tonight, so I think I'll get the fire going good, and it'll be cozy as a bug in a rug tomorrow morning when everybody comes."

It certainly was a pretty horse, and he certainly knew how to ride him; and the big beautiful brown saddle and Mr. Black's riding habit made me wish I had a big brown horse and a riding outfit and could go galloping around all over Sugar Creek territory.

Almost right away, we all decided to play outdoors awhile, 'cause if there was going to be a real cold wave tonight, it meant that tomorrow we'd all have to stay inside the school most of the time, 'cause sometimes a cold wave in Sugar Creek territory meant twenty degrees below zero. Poetry went in the house and got his binoculars and we all climbed up on their chicken house which didn't have any snow on its roof, and started to look around Sugar Creek at different things. Little Jim grinned when he noticed there wasn't any snow on the roof of the chicken house, and said, "That certainly was a good sermon this morning." Then he grunted and sat down astride the chicken-house roof, right close to a little tin chimney out of which white smoke was coming, there being a kerosene heater inside the chicken house.

"It sure was," Poetry said, with the binoculars focused in the direction Mr. Black had gone.

"Here, Bill, look at him, will you—he's stopping at Circus's house. Suppose maybe he's going to take a picture of one of Circus's sisters?"

Dragonfly giggled when Poetry said that, and I felt hot inside because Circus had a lot of sisters, and one of them was a real honest-to-goodness girl who wasn't afraid of mice or spiders, and sometimes I carried her dinner pail to school. I knew Dragonfly was trying to tease me, so I said, "Here, let me see."

A jiffy later I was looking at Mr. Black stopping his big horse at Circus's house. Just that second, Dragonfly shoved his hands against my knees behind me, and both my knees buckled, and I swung around a little. When I looked again toward Circus's house, the binoculars were focused not on his house but on our red-brick schoolhouse farther across the field. All of a sudden I let out a gasp and a yell, and felt a queer feeling inside of me. For right there on the north side of the schoolhouse was a ladder leaning up against the eaves and— yes, I could see it as plain as day, there was something that looked like a flat board lying right across the top of the schoolhouse chimney.

It was even plainer than day what had happened, and that was that Shorty Long and Bob Till had been to our house and barn while we were in church and had stolen Snow-white and some other pigeons and then, seeing how nice and light and easy it was to carry Dad's new ladder, and remembering the story of *The Hoosier Schoolmaster*, and both of the boys not liking the Sugar Creek Gang, and Shorty Long especially not liking me terribly much, they had borrowed the ladder and had used it to put the board on the chimney, so Mr. Black would be smoked out when he started the fire, and I, Bill Collins, and maybe all the Sugar Creek Gang, would get into even more trouble with Mr. Black.

I was thinking all those worried thoughts in less than a jiffy while I was looking through those binoculars, and was still standing on the roof of Poetry's dad's chicken house, with Poetry and Little Jim beside me.

I must have let out a very excited gasp, 'cause Poetry said, "'Smatter, Bill?"

Little Jim said in his mouselike voice which

was also excited for a change, "See anything important?"

Dragonfly was on the ground in front of me and he yelled up and said, "What's the matter?" Then he sneezed, which is what people sometimes do when all of a sudden they look up and the sun gets into their eyes, which it did in Dragonfly's eyes right that second.

"Quick!" I yelled to the gang. "Come on, we've got to get to the schoolhouse before Mr. Black does or the schoolhouse will catch on fire maybe." The ladder was on the side of the schoolhouse where I knew Mr. Black wouldn't see it when he got there. I whirled around, made a leap for the ground, landed in a snowdrift, got out of it in a hurry, and raced as fast as I could down Poetry's lane toward the highway.

Poetry and Dragonfly and Little Jim came whizzing along behind me, yelling what was the matter and why was I in such a hurry, and how on earth could the schoolhouse catch on fire, and why did we have to get there before Mr. Black did.

I still had Poetry's binoculars in my hand and was running, panting, dodging drifts, and all the time I could see in my mind's eye Dad's new ladder leaning up against the schoolhouse. I knew that if Mr. Black ever saw it and found out whose it was, I'd have a hard time explaining it to him that I hadn't done it.

In between pants, I managed to get it into the heads of the rest of the gang what I'd seen, and why I was in a hurry. "We've got to get there first and get that board off the chimney or the room will be filled with smoke and maybe there will be an explosion." I remembered that in *The Hoosier Schoolmaster* there had really been *some* smoke.

Poetry, who was my best friend, was almost as mad as I was, and he said behind me between his short breaths, "Those dirty bums! They're the cause of *all* our trouble with our new teacher!"

And would you believe it? Little Jim, who heard him say that, yelled to us, "Are you sure?" Imagine him not being sure.

We took a shortcut we knew about. Once when we were on the top of a little hill in Dragonfly's woods, we stopped and Poetry and I took a couple of quick looks through his binoculars toward Circus's house to see if Mr. Black was still there. His horse was, so we guessed he was too.

I saw him out in their backyard and a whole flock of girls was lined up against their woodshed and he was taking their picture. I didn't see Circus there anywhere, and I wished he was with us because he could run faster than any of us and also climb better.

"Come on!" I yelled to the rest of the guys with me. "We can make it, I think." Away we went.

"Wait!" Dragonfly yelled from pretty far back.

"I'm out of breath. I—can't—can't run so—fast!" which he couldn't.

All of a sudden Poetry stopped and said, "We're crazy, Bill, we can't make it. Look! There he goes now, right straight toward the schoolhouse. Quick! Drop down! He's looking this way."

He ducked behind a rail fence which is where we were at the time, and I dropped down beside him. Dragonfly was still coming along not more than fifty feet behind us, with little Jim staying back with him.

I hated to stop, and I hated to have to realize what was happening. But it was true that Mr. Black was going to get to the schoolhouse first and he'd start the fire in the schoolhouse stove because he wouldn't see the ladder 'cause it was on the opposite side of the school from the woodshed where he kept his kindling wood.

I'd seen Mr. Black start fires in the Poetry-shaped iron stove before. He always went straight to the corner of the schoolhouse under the long shelf where we all kept our dinner pails, and pick up a tin can of kerosene which he kept in the corner, and in which he kept some neat little sticks. Those little sticks would be all soaked with kerosene from having been there all night or longer, and he'd take them to the stove and lay them in carefully, along with other small pieces of wood and a few larger pieces, and then he would very carefully light a match and touch the flame to the kerosene-soaked sticks, and right away there would be a nice fire.

I knew it would take Mr. Black only a little while to lay the fire, and in a few minutes the fire in the stove would be roaring away. But with the board on the chimney, the smoke couldn't get out. It'd have to come out of the stove somewhere, and the schoolhouse would be filled with smoke in a jiffy. Also I remembered that the Christmas tree which we'd left up since Christmas wasn't more than fifteen feet from the stove, and its needles were dry enough to burn.

Something had to be done in a hurry, and yet there was Mr. Black getting closer and closer to the schoolhouse. In fact, it was already too late to get there without being seen before he went inside. I knew that if I got there in time to hurry up that ladder and take off the board, I'd have to do it *after* Mr. Black got inside, and before he could get the fire laid and started.

The rail fence behind which we were hiding right that minute was on the same side of the school the ladder was, and about as far from the school as our barn is from our house.

All of us were squatted down behind the fence now, and I took charge of the gang and said, "You guys stay here. The very minute he gets in, I'll dive out of here and make a beeline for the schoolhouse, and zip up the ladder and take the board off. Then

I'll climb back down, take the ladder and drag it around behind the schoolhouse quick, and come back here. Then tonight or sometime after Mr. Black goes home, some of us'll sneak over and bring the ladder home, and everything'll be all right."

It was a good idea if only it would work, which it had to, or I just knew that the gentleman I'd made up my mind I was going to try to be, would get a terrible licking, which any gentleman shouldn't have to have, or he isn't one, which I wasn't yet—

"Let *me* do it," Poetry said beside me, puffing hard from the fast run we'd just had.

Dragonfly said, "The ladder'd break with you on it," trying to be funny and not being.

Little Jim piped up and said, "All the snow's off the roof right next to the chimney." I looked at him real quick, and he had a far-away look in his eyes, like he was not only looking at the dry roof all around the schoolhouse chimney, but was thinking something very important, which he'd heard in church that morning, but which I hadn't.

"Here goes," I said, my heart beating wildly. "You guys stay here, and watch."

Little Jim piped up and said, "We will—we'll watch and—and—" I knew what he was going to say even before he said it, and for some reason it seemed like it was all right for him to say it, and it didn't sound sissified for him to either. While I was climbing over that rail fence and making a dive for

96

the schoolhouse and the ladder, Little Jim's whole sentence was tumbling around in my mind, and it was, "We will—we'll watch and—and *pray*."

Little Jim was almost as good a friend of mine as Tom Till was, I thought.

A jiffy later I reached my dad's new ladder and started to start up when I heard somebody running behind me and saying in a husky whisper, "Hey, Bill! Stop. Wait! Let me hold the ladder."

I looked around quick and it was Poetry behind me, and I knew he was right. My dad had taught me never to go up a ladder until I was sure the bottom of it was safely set so it wouldn't slip, or unless somebody stayed at the bottom to hold it so it couldn't.

A jiffy later I was on my way up, and in another jifly I was at the eaves. Being a very good climber, I scrambled up the other little ladder that was made out of nailed-on boards, to the red-brick chimney. I had to be as quiet as I could though because of not wanting Mr. Black to hear me on the roof. I also was going to have to be careful when I took the board off so the sound of it sliding off wouldn't go down the chimney through the stove.

In another jiffy I'd have had the board off, and have given it a toss far out where it wouldn't have hit Poetry, and then I'd have been on my way down again. But when I took hold of the wide, flat board, I couldn't any more get it off than anything. I gasped out loud when I saw why I couldn't get it off. There was a nail driven into each end of it, and a piece of stovepipe wire was wrapped around the head of each nail. Then the wire was twisted around and around the brick chimney, down where it was smaller, and that crazy old board wouldn't budge— an almost *new* board, rather, and as soon as I saw it, I knew it was the board out of the swing which we have in the walnut tree at our house. *Why, the dirty crooks!* I thought. They wanted it to be *sure* to look like Bill Collins put it up here.

I was holding onto the chimney, in fact I was sort of behind it, so I wouldn't slide down. I could hear sounds down in the schoolhouse of somebody doing something to the stove, which must have been Mr. Black finishing laying the fire, 'cause right that second I heard a sound like an iron door closing on the big, round, iron, Poetry-shaped stove and, almost a second later, a puff of bluish smoke came bursting out through a crack where the board didn't quite cover the chimney on one side, and I knew that the fire was started. I knew that in a few jiffies that one-room school would be filled with smoke, and a mad teacher would come storming out to see what on earth was the matter with the chimney, and I'd be in for it.

"Hey!" I hissed down to Poetry, shielding my voice with my hand so the sound would go toward

98

Poetry instead of down the chimney. Poetry heard me and dived out far enough from the schoolhouse to see me, and I hissed to him, "It's too late. The fire's already started. What'll I do? I can't get it off. They've wired it on. If I had a pair of pliers, I could cut the wire."

And Poetry yelled up to me and said, "There's a pair in the schoolhouse."

Awful sounds came up the chimney from down inside the schoolhouse, and I could just imagine what Mr. Black was thinking, and maybe was saying too. Smoke was pouring out of the chimney beside my face, but I knew the crack was too small for *all* the smoke to get out, and the room down there would be filling up with smoke.

What on earth to do, was screaming at me in my mind—

Then Poetry had an idea and it was, "Come on down quick, and let's run. Let's leave the ladder and everything!"

"But it's my dad's ladder, and it's our swing board, out of our walnut tree swing."

"I say, let's *run!*" Poetry half yelled and half hissed up to me and, for some reason, knowing I couldn't get the board off the chimney, and guessing what might happen if I got caught, it seemed like Poetry's idea was as good as any. So I turned and started to scoot my way down the board ladder on the roof to the ladder Poetry would be holding for me. Then—well, I don't know how it happened, but my boot slipped before I could get my feet on dad's ladder. I felt all of me slipping toward the edge of the roof—slipping, slipping, slipping, and I knew I wouldn't be able to stop myself. In a jiffy I'd be going slippety-sizzle over the edge of the eaves and land with a wham at Poetry's feet. I might even land on him and hurt him. Even while I was sliding, I heard a sickening sound in the schoolhouse somewhere, like a stove was falling down, or a chair was falling over or something. Then my feet were over the edge, and I was grasping and grasping with my bare hands at the slippery roof; and they couldn't find anything to hold onto. Then I heard another sound that was even more sickening than the one I'd heard in the schoolhouse, and it was a ripping and tearing sound. Then I felt a long sharp pain on me somewhere and I knew my trousers had caught on a nail or something.

R-r-r-ip! R-r-r-ip! Tear-r-r! And I knew that when I would hit the ground in a few half jiffies, there would be a big hole in my trousers which I'd have to explain to Mom when I got home, as well as a lot of other things to both Mom and Dad.

The next thing I knew I was off the edge and falling, and the very next thing I learned awful quick was that I had landed ker-wham-thud in a snow drift at the foot of the ladder.

10

EVEN WHILE I WAS FALLING and scared and feeling the long sharp pain running up and down my hip where I'd probably been scratched by a nail, I was wondering what would happen next— what Mr. Black would do, and what would happen when I got home, and also I was wondering how bad I would be hurt when I fell—and then I lit ker-fluffety-sizzle in that big snowdrift.

And there I was, Bill Collins, the one member of the Sugar Creek Gang who had made up his mind he wasn't going to have anything to do with smoking a teacher out of his schoolhouse. The one who was going to be what is called a gentleman was now lying upside down in a scrambled-up heap, with one of my trouser legs ripped maybe halfway down, and I was all covered with snow and with my mind all tangled up and everything.

The fall didn't hurt much though because the snowdrift was pretty deep, but we had to do something and do it quick.

Just that minute, I heard the schoolhouse door open around in front. While I was trying to scramble to my feet, I looked toward the front of the school. Right that second Mr. Black came swishing around to our side of the schoolhouse with a big pail in his hand and swooped with it down onto a snowdrift, scooped up a pailful of snow and, without even looking in our direction, dived back around the corner of the schoolhouse like he was half scared to death. Right that second Poetry yelled to Dragonfly and Little Jim, who were still hiding behind the rail fence, "Hurry up! I think the schoolhouse is on fire inside! Let's go help Mr. Black put it out."

And so I, Bill Collins, an imaginary gentleman, but not looking like even half a one, staggered out of my snowdrift. The four of us made a dive for the front of the schoolhouse and around to the open door, which had smoke pouring out of it, to see if we could help Mr. Black put out the fire, if there was one.

"I can't go in," Dragonfly said. "I'm allergic to smoke. It'll make me sneeze."

Just that second we heard Mr. Black's horse, which was tied at the front gate, snort and make crazy horse noises. Even before I could imagine what was going to happen, it had happened. There was a noise like a leather strap straining, and then a cracking and splintering sound. I looked just in time to see the little wooden gate, to which the horse had been tied, break in two or maybe three, and part of it go galloping down the road being dragged by a scared wild-eyed saddle horse. At the same time I saw a half-wild-looking man come running out of the smoking schoolhouse and make a wild dash through the place where the gate had been and go racing after the horse, not even seeing us boys. Or if he saw us, he didn't pay any attention to us, but yelled to Prince in a commanding voice, *"Whoa! Whoa!"*

It certainly was an exciting minute. In spite of the way I knew I must have looked myself, with snow all over me and with a ripped trouser leg and everything, Mr. Black looked even worse as he went racing down the road after his horse, yelling for him to stop. The very minute he went swishing past us, I noticed that his hands were black with soot, as was his face, and he really looked like a wild man. For some reason, even while everything else was all topsy-turvy in my mind, I couldn't help but remember Poetry's poetry:

The Sugar Creek Gang had the worst of teachers,
And "Black" his name was called,
His round red face had the homeliest of features,
He was fat and forty and bald.

Only his face was black as well as his name, and I knew if he hadn't been bald, his hair would certainly have been mussed up like mine is most of the time when my hat is off. Only Mr. Black's fur hat was still on.

Say, Prince certainly wasn't in any horse mood to stop, because of being scared, I suppose. what with the smoke pouring out of the schoolhouse, and all the noise which the stove had made, and with the gang making a noise and running excitedly, and everything. That horse with a gate tied to its bridle rein probably was as scared as a dog or cat is when a boy that ought to know better ties a can to its tail and shouldn't and it gets scared and runs, and keeps on running—

Prince kept running and the piece of gate kept swinging in different directions. Every time the horse turned his head this way or that, the gate would swing around and sock him in the side and scare him maybe even worse. I thought how terrible it would be if Prince would get his feet all tangled up in part of the gate and fall, and maybe break one of his legs and have to be killed. That is what nearly always has to be done to a horse when it breaks one of its legs because you can't get a horse to be quiet for weeks and months long enough for its leg to heal. I certainly wouldn't want such a pretty horse to have to be killed.

There we were—the four of us, innocent-faced Little Jim, dragonfly-eyed Dragonfly, barrel-shaped Poetry, and me, red-haired, freckle-faced Bill Collins. And there was Mr. Black and his horse getting farther and farther up the road that leads past Circus's and Big Jim's houses, which are on the other side of the road from each other.

But we couldn't stand there and just watch a runaway horse with a man chasing it when a schoolhouse was on fire, or was supposed to be. I'd been so excited about the runaway horse that I'd almost forgotten the schoolhouse.

I turned around quick to the door, and would you believe it? Little Jim and Poetry and Dragonfly were already inside and I'd been standing out there by what used to be a gate, watching Mr. Black and his horse all by myself! Even Dragonfly was inside although he had opened one of the windows and was standing leaning halfway out and breathing fresh air so he wouldn't sneeze, because he was allergic to smoke. That schoolhouse certainly looked funny with the sunlight, which came in the windows, shining through the bluish smoke, so that things at first weren't very clear to my eyes. But when about a half jiffy later my eyes were accustomed to the dark light, I saw a really crazy-looking schoolhouse. There on the teacher's desk, upside down, was the teacher's great big swivel chair; and the brooms and the mop were piled on top of that, and written in great big letters with chalk on the blackboard, was Poetry's poem about a teacher not having any hair. The old Christmas tree which had been standing so pretty and straight in a corner of the platform was lying on the floor, and the popcorn and paper chains which the Sugar Creek pupils had made were in a tangled-up mess all over the tree and the floor. The stove door was open and the firebox was half filled with snow, which maybe Mr. Black had scooped in to put out the fire he'd started awhile ago.

All that mess, with the turned-over tree and Poetry's poem and the topsy-turvy desk and chair, meant that those two boys had not only put the board across the chimney but had crawled into the schoolhouse through one of the windows maybe and upset things, then had printed the poem there for our teacher to see and—well, you can guess I wasn't feeling very much like a gentleman. I knew that if Shorty Long and Bob Till were right there right that minute I'd probably prove to them that I wasn't one either.

It was Little Jim who woke us all up that something had to be done. We were all sort of standing helpless, looking around at the mess, when he piped up and said in a voice that sounded like he was the leader of the gang, "Hey, you guys! Let's *do* something, before he gets back. Let's straighten things up, and maybe when he comes he'll believe that we didn't do it!"

Then Dragonfly whirled around from his window, and said, "They're clear down to Circus's house already, and the horse just turned into their barnyard," which made me want to make a dive for the window to look too.

But I didn't because all of a sudden Little Jim said something else: "Let's start the fire for him real quick, and that'll show him we like him."

That started my mind to working. "We can't," I said. "The board's still across the chimney and we can't get it off."

That started Poetry to thinking and he made a heavy dive for the long shelf along the back wall. Right there where they had been, only there was some stovepipe wire beside them, were the pliers. In a jiffy Poetry and I were back outside and, with him holding the ladder and with me all trembling inside but not too nervous to climb, I went up that ladder, hand over hand, and in less than a half-dozen worried jiffies, had our swing board off the chimney and tossed it into a snowdrift. When I was down again, Poetry and I whisked the ladder back behind the schoolhouse and, with our feet, covered it and the swing board with snow. When we got back inside the schoolhouse, Little Jim and Dragonfly had used their hands and the little fire shovel and scooped as much of the snow out of the stove as they could. They had laid the fire again, like we all knew how to do, from having seen our parents do it. Poetry shoved his hand in his pocket for his waterproof matchbox, and in a little while we had a roaring fire in the big round iron stove.

107

Then all of us started cleaning up the schoolhouse as fast as we could.

Poetry grabbed an eraser and, as quick and as fierce as a cat jumping on a mouse, leaped toward the blackboard and swished his poetry into nothing. Little Jim found a dustcloth and went up one row of seats and down another, carefully dusting each one just like I imagine he'd been taught at home—not swishing the cloth around too fast, which would make more dust. I began to try to untangle the Christmas tree from the popcorn strings and paper chains, thinking how nice the tree would look standing in the corner again. All of a sudden Dragonfly hissed, "Hey everybody! Come here, quick! See what I found!"

Dragonfly had been standing by a wide-open window because there was still too much smoke in the room for him to breathe without sneezing. The Sugar Creek School's great big unabridged dictionary was wide open on a shelf which was fastened to the wall by the window.

Before we could get there, Dragonfly said excitedly, "It's Mr. Black's diary!"

Well, if there is anything a person wants to read, and shouldn't and must not, it's somebody's diary, unless that person tells him to. My parents had told me that when I was little, and Dad had licked me once for reading his, and so I knew Dragonfly shouldn't have read Mr. Black's diary. So when I got to where he was and saw him looking at a pretty leather-bound notebook lying flat open on the big open dictionary, I said, "Stop reading that! It's not good etiquette," which is not good manners or something.

I certainly wasn't going to turn any pages of the diary and read them, I said to myself, remembering what my parents had told me, and also the half-hard licking my dad had given me for reading his when he told me not to. But when I got to where Dragonfly was and looked to see if it really was Mr. Black's diary, without even trying to I saw on the page that was half open, written in printed letters, these words:

The Sugar Creek Gang had the worst of teachers,
And "Black" his name was called;

For some reason it didn't look very funny. In fact, it seemed like anybody who had first thought up such a poem must have been crazy in the head.

I knew I shouldn't have been reading, and I decided to quit quick, which I did. Only I saw one other thing just as my eyes were leaving the page, and it was:

Things have come to a showdown with the boys. I know I'm going to have to take drastic action soon."

"What's 'drastic' mean?" Dragonfly wanted to know, just as I turned away.

109

I knew he'd read what I'd read, so I said, "I don't know, but whatever it is, I'll bet it'll hurt like everything." I reached out my hand and laid it down flat on the opened diary, so I wouldn't read anything else.

Then Dragonfly said, "Psst! Listen!"

We all listened for a half jiffy and things were so quiet in that still half-smokey room we could hear only the crackling of the fire in the stove. All of a sudden there was a step on the schoolhouse porch, and the door was thrust open. There stood Mr. Black himself, looking right straight at us.

11

WELL, WHEN FOUR BOYS get caught doing something they're not sure they're supposed to be doing, they don't know what to do or what to say. Sometimes they start talking right away to explain *why* they are doing what they're doing—which is what *we* started to do. That is, *we started to,* but all of us talking at once didn't make sense, so we stopped. This is what we all said though: Dragonfly said, "Good morning, Mr. Black!" which is what you say to a teacher when it *is* morning and you are trying to be polite. Poetry said, "Somebody wrote a crazy poem about you on the black, Mr. Blackboard, and I erased it." Little Jim said, "That certainly was a good sermon this morning, Mr. Black." And I, William Jasper Collins, with my torn trousers and my freckled face and my rumpled red hair and my mussed-up mind said, "I hope you don't have to shoot him if he broke his leg. He didn't break it, did he?"

All of us said most of these things at the same

time, while we were standing in a semicircle around the unabridged dictionary with the open notebook on it.

Mr. Black was puffing and panting, he being Poetry-shaped as well as the stove, but all of a sudden he said. "Wait, boys, don't move! I want to get your pictures right where you are, and *as* you are." Before we could decide to move or not to move, he whirled around, hurried over toward the shelf where we always set our dinner pails on school days, and came back with his camera which we hadn't noticed had been there. It was a very pretty camera and was the kind people used when they took a flashbulb picture.

What on earth he wanted a picture of us for, I didn't know, unless it was so he could prove to anybody who didn't believe it, that we were a bunch of roughnecks. Quick as a blinding flash he had our picture taken, and then he whirled around like he wanted to take some more pictures. He stopped and stared at the Christmas tree which I had stood back up in the corner, with the popcorn and paper chains tangled up on it, and at the erased blackboard and at his desk which didn't have any chairs upside down on it. He said, "Who straightened up this room! Did you boys do that?"

"Yes, sir," I said, "we did; we wanted to prove to you that we didn't do it."

"You *what!*"

"We wanted to prove to you that we didn't *do* it!" Little Jim said.

Mr. Black looked at Little Jim and at all of us like he thought we were even crazier than we felt, and he said, "Prove you didn't do *what?*"

"That we didn't put the board across the—*ouch!*" Dragonfly started to talk but stopped his sentence with an *ouch* when I quick kicked him on the shin.

Mr. Black's eyes opened wide. Then for the first time he seemed to notice that the fire was going again and that the stove wasn't smoking. So he scratched his head above his left ear, hurried over to the stove with the camera in his hand, set his camera on his big desk, opened the stove's door and shut it again, and just stood there, looking first at the stove and then at us. I wished I knew what he was thinking; then I noticed that his eyes glanced off in the direction of the blackboard and to the beech switches which were lying on a ledge at the top. I could just see myself and all of us getting a licking in about seven jiffies. I started to edge toward the door, but he must have guessed what I was thinking, 'cause he barked a command, "William Collins! Stop where you are!"

I stopped stock-still, trembling inside of me, wondering what the word "drastic" was going to mean.

Then Mr. Black barked to me, "Go to the blackboard and get me those beech switches!" There was a tone of voice in his words which made me start toward the blackboard instead of toward the only door the schoolhouse had. I had to pass Dragonfly's open window which was still open because there was still some smoke in the room. It would have been easy for me to make a dive out of that window, but I didn't want to leave the gang alone there with an angry teacher. I also had to pass close to the unabridged dictionary, and I all of a sudden decided if I knew what the word "drastic" meant, it might give me an idea what to do next. So I stopped and quick turned the pages to the letter *D* and was trying to find "drastic" when Mr. Black barked a question, "Young man! *What are you doing?*"

I jumped like I had been shot, but made myself say as calmly as I could, over my shoulder, "I just wanted to look up an important word first. I'll get the switches in just a minute."

"If the word is *punishment*," Mr. Black said to me angrily, "it's a *noun*, and it means *beech switches*. You bring them to me!" And I knew I had to do it. I stopped looking in the dictionary and, feeling simply terrible inside of me because of not having done anything wrong on purpose, but knowing Mr. Black wouldn't believe us even if we told him, I got the switches and took them toward him. But I was so nervous I dropped one of them.

Say, Little Jim who is very quick when he makes up his mind to do something, made a dive for the floor, picked up the switch I'd dropped and quick

114

took the other one out of my hand, and handed them both to Mr. Black and said to him very politely, "Here you are, sir, with all the old brown dead leaves gone—every one of them."

"What on *earth?*" I thought, and looked at Little Jim's face and then at Mr. Black's.

Say, our teacher's face had all of a sudden the queerest expression on it, and he looked at Little Jim like he wondered what on earth himself. Then he looked at me, and his face was hard again.

Right that second I remembered my torn trousers, and the place where they were torn clear through to the skin. The scratch was still hurting, so I said, "If you're—if you're going to lick me, d-don't hit me on my scratched thigh!" I turned sidewise to him, stooped over part way, and showed him my torn trousers and the reddish scratch on my thigh, which for some reason didn't look half as bad as I wished it did right at that minute.

Mr. Black frowned, and asked fast, "Where'd you get that scratch?"

Dragonfly said, "When he was up on the—*ouch!*" I stopped Dragonfly with a kick on his shin again.

"What's that? Where'd you say he got it?" Mr. Black barked his question to Dragonfly.

And before any of us could stop him, Dragonfly had said, "On the schoolhouse roof."

I just couldn't believe Dragonfly was that dumb—that he didn't know he oughtn't to tell where I'd gotten that scratch. I remembered with a mad thought that we'd had trouble with Dragonfly once before because he had been friends with Shorty Long.

There wasn't any time to think or to remember anything else Dragonfly had done, but it certainly didn't feel good to have one of our own gang be a tattletale. Why, he was supposed to be one of my very best friends!

I looked at Little Jim and Poetry to see what they thought and to see if they could think of anything that might help us from getting a licking with those leafless beech switches. Poetry had a pucker on his forehead like he was thinking, or maybe trying to, and Little Jim had that innocent lamblike look on his small face which, when he looks like that, always reminds me of the picture his mom has on the wall above their piano in their house, of the Good Shepherd with a little lamb in his arms, with the Good Shepherd's hand on the little lamb's poll, which is the top of its head.

Then in a flash I was seeing Mr. Black again standing with one hand on his hip and the other holding onto one of the beech switches, he having laid the other switch down on Sylvia's little sister's desk, which was beside and behind him.

"And *what*," Mr. Black said to me, "were you doing on the schoolhouse *roof?*"

Well, I hated to tell him because I thought he wouldn't believe it. And another reason I hated to tell him was because if I did, it would mean I'd have to tell him somebody *else* had put the board *on* the chimney, and that wouldn't be fair to Little Tom Till who was Bob's brother. And my mom was trying to get Shorty Long's mom to be a Christian, and I hated to be a tattletale about Shorty and Bob. So I just stood there without answering Mr. Black.

"Answer me!" he demanded. I could see he was getting really angry. I took one quick look at the door to see if I could dive past him and get there first and make a wild dash for home. I saw Little Jim's face and it reminded me again of the Bible picture above his piano, and that reminded me of a Bible verse I'd memorized, which was, "A soft answer turneth away wrath." Then I thought of Mr. Black's pretty horse and said politely, "Your horse is the prettiest horse I ever saw. I hope he didn't fall and break his leg."

I looked at Poetry and he winked at me, and said to Mr. Black, "It'll get dark pretty soon and if there's going to be a cold wave tonight, we'd better help you carry in plenty of wood. We'll help you bank the fire good."

But it was Little Jim who saved us from trouble when he said, "That was a good sermon this morning, wasn't it, Mr. Black? All of us are going to try not to be mad at you anymore; and if we've done anything wrong, we're sorry. We hope you won't

117

give us a licking, but if you do, we won't even get mad."

Mr. Black looked down at that innocent-looking little face, and kept on looking at it. Then he seemed to get a faraway expression in his eyes like he was thinking about something that wasn't in the schoolhouse. I noticed his hand that had the switch in it was trembling, and I knew he was really mad because my hands sometimes shake when I feel that way.

Then he looked like he was hearing something outside and, without saying anything, turned and, with the switches in his hands, walked with heavy steps over to the window and looked out, with his back to us. I could hear him breathing heavily like he had been running, and there was a terrible feeling inside of me, which is the way a boy feels when he knows some grownup person is awful angry.

The four of us stood by the stove and looked at different things, not any of us moving, and not a one of us looking at each other, except I glanced at different ones of us out of the corner of my eye, and then looked away again. I could still hear Mr. Black breathing heavily. I didn't look, but I guessed he was still standing and looking out into the late afternoon sunlight on the snow.

Then I heard him cough a little and clear his throat, and heard him walking. I looked and he was going to the blackboard where, very carefully, like

118

he was afraid he'd drop one of them, he laid the beech switches on the shelf. Then he turned and sat down in his chair at his desk and picked up a book that was lying there, opened it and leafed through it slowly.

What on earth! I thought.

You could have knocked me over with a turkey feather when I saw the kind of book he was leafing through. I'd never seen it there on that desk before, and I wondered where it had come from. But there it was as plain as day, an honest-to-goodness great big beautiful brown-bound Bible.

All of us were so quiet, and I had such a tense feeling inside of me that I couldn't say a word, and didn't want to anyway. The fingers of one of Mr. Black's hands were sort of drumming on the desk, and he was looking at something in the very front of the Bible in the place where people nearly always write their names to show whose Bible it is.

Then he began to turn the pages slowly, not looking up at any of us, but like he was thinking about something that wasn't in the schoolroom. I could hear the crackling of the fire in the stove, and hear us all breathing. I caught a corner of Poetry's eye with a corner of one of mine, but couldn't tell what he was thinking. Little Jim had his small hands stretched out in front of him warming them at the stove, and Dragonfly was trying to get his father's big red bandanna handkerchief out of his pocket

119

before he would sneeze about something, but didn't get it out quick enough and the sneeze showered itself on the hot stove and made a sizzling sound.

Dragonfly grabbed his nose with the red handkerchief and stopped most of the next sneeze, so only a little tail of it exploded.

The fingers of both of Mr. Black's hands were drumming on the desk on each side of his open Bible, and he had his eyes glued to the page, although I could tell the way he was staring at the page that he maybe wasn't reading but only thinking.

It was as quiet, in fact ten times as quiet, as if we were having school.

A jiffy later I heard Mr. Black clear his throat and say to us, "It's been a very exciting afternoon, boys, and I don't feel any too well. I think I ran too hard to catch Prince."

He took a very deep breath and sighed and yawned and leaned back in his chair, without looking straight at us but just in our direction, just as Little Jim piped up and said, "Did you catch him? Was he hurt?"

"Circus stopped him," Mr. Black said, "and we put him up in their barn till he calms down and quits trembling. You boys want to bring in a couple of armloads of wood?"

Well, in a few jiffies all of us boys were carrying in wood and stacking it in the back of the schoolroom where we would have plenty to keep the schoolhouse nice and warm tomorrow.

I just couldn't figure it out—our not getting any licking, and Mr. Black reading the Bible and all of a sudden acting very kind. Why, when we carried in our loads of wood, he acted like he was our very best friend, and that we not only hadn't done anything wrong, but that he didn't even *think* we had. I couldn't understand it, but all the time Little Jim had a happy grin on his face while we worked, and he kept saying, "I thought it would work. I was pretty sure it would, and it did."

"What worked?" I said to him, just as he opened the door for me and I went in with an armload of wood, and he shut the door after me. Dragonfly and Poetry were out in the woodshed getting another load.

"Oh, something," Little Jim said, and wouldn't tell me, but he certainly had a cheerful expression on his face.

Pretty soon when we were all done and were getting ready to go home, Mr. Black stopped us and said, "Wait a minute, boys, I need one more picture. You know, next Wednesday night Mrs. Mansfield is going to give a book review of *The Hoosier Schoolmaster* at the Literary Society and I've promised to illustrate the story on the screen with some modern pictures from real life. I ought to have one of a teacher putting a board on the

121

chimney of a schoolhouse. Leslie, you get that ladder I saw you boys carry behind the schoolhouse awhile ago, and set it up again—here, Bill, hold my Bible a minute." He thrust the beautiful new brown-bound Bible in my hands and started around the schoolhouse with Poetry to where we'd buried the ladder.

"What on *earth!*" I thought, and decided he must have looked toward the schoolhouse once and seen us putting it there, while he was down the road between the schoolhouse and Circus's house.

Without hardly knowing I was going to, I quick opened the Bible to the first blank page and what I saw was, "To my dear son, Sam Black, from Mother." And right below it were printed, very carefully, the words:

This Book will keep you from sin,
or
Sin will keep you from this Book.

In a jiffy the ladder was set up, with Little Jim and me holding it, and Mr. Black on his way up. Poetry, who knew how to take pictures better than any of the rest of us, was standing out from the schoolhouse, and he snapped the picture.

While Mr. Black was still up on the roof, he called down to all of us in a cheerful voice, "That was a very clever poem you boys composed—you know, the one you had on the snowman yesterday, and on the blackboard this afternoon. I think I got a very good picture of both of them for next Wednesday night—the people of Sugar Creek will think it very clever. When I first got the idea of illustrating the book review for Mrs. Mansfield, I didn't know how much cooperation you boys were going to give me."

Things still didn't make sense—I couldn't understand it.

On the way home though, with Poetry and me carrying Dad's new light ladder and with Little Jim carrying our swing board, all of a sudden Dragonfly let out a yell and made a dive for something shining in the road, swooped down on it and picked it up, and exclaimed, *"Good luck!* No wonder we had good luck! Here's a brand new horseshoe! No wonder we didn't get a lickin' from Mr. Black."

And it was! I knew it must have come off Prince when he was running down this very same road about an hour ago with half a gate swinging on his bridle rein.

Dragonfly hung the new horseshoe on his arm and said excitedly, "Will my mother ever be tickled! She'll hang it above our kitchen door. We've got three there now I found *last* year, and this is my first one *this year*. Boy oh boy, it's going to be a lucky year for the Sugar Creek Gang!"

Little Jim, who had been shuffling along ahead of the rest of us with the swing board under one arm and with his stick in his other hand, stopped all of a sudden and looked back over our heads toward where the sun had just gone behind a cloud in the southwest, and he had a faraway expression in his eyes. He didn't pay any attention to what Dragonfly had said, but dropped back beside me and said, "That certainly was a swell sermon this morning. I knew maybe Sylvia's dad was going to preach about that, and sure enough he did."

"About *what?*" I asked him, Little Jim being the only one of the gang that it was easy to talk with about sermons, except maybe Poetry.

Little Jim socked at a brown mullein stalk with his stick and scattered brown seeds in different directions, then he answered me with his back still turned, "Oh, about when you get Jesus in your heart, you don't get mad so easy, and when you do, you behave yourself anyway—just like a fire in a house melts the snow off the roof. Or like when spring comes, the new leaves will push all of the old dead leaves off that've hung on all winter."

Just that second Poetry, who had the other end of the ladder, yelled back to me, "Quit walking so jerkily, Bill Collins!"

Then I remembered that our teacher had been in church that morning, and of course he had heard the part of the sermon I hadn't heard because I had been thinking about Poetry's pet lamb and Snow-white, our white pigeon.

124

Then Little Jim said, "When I put that question in 'The Minister's Question Box,' just inside the church door this morning, I hoped Sylvia's dad would answer it in his very first sermon, and he did."

So that was it! It was as plain as day to me now. Dragonfly spoke up then: "Was that what you were thinking about yesterday afternoon when you were looking up in the beech tree at the bottom of Bumblebee hill, and when you kept talking about snow on people's houses?" And that was the first time I even guessed that that little spindle-legged guy knew what we were talking about.

"Sure," Little Jim said.

Dragonfly tossed his new horseshoe up in the air and caught it when it came down. He said, "It's a pretty horseshoe, anyway—besides, I bet the gang *does* have a lucky year, don't you?"

Little Jim whispered to me something that was a real secret, and it made me like him awful well, to know he wasn't afraid to talk to me about it. It was, "Do you suppose Mr. Black *really* became a Christian this morning while Sylvia's dad was preaching —or maybe he is just *going* to let Jesus into his heart real soon?"

"I don't know," I said.

Poetry, who didn't know what we were all talking about because he was up at the other end of the kind of long ladder, said back to us, "We shouldn't have carried this ladder home. We should have made

Shorty Long and Bob Till do it. They took it there in the first place!"

And Little Jim piped up, "Are you sure? Maybe Mr. Black did it so he could get a picture of it for next Wednesday night."

Dragonfly heard that and said, "But who piled the chairs up on his desk and knocked the Christmas tree over and everything?"

"Yeah, that's right," Little Jim said. "I guess maybe they did do it, but I'm not very mad at 'em."

"I'm not either," I said, "not *very* much anyway." And I wasn't—only I knew that as long as they lived in the neighborhood we could expect most anything to happen.

Then Little Jim said to all of us, "As soon as the new cold wave is over, I'll bet it'll start to get warm. And pretty soon spring'll be here, and all the beech switches all along Sugar Creek will have new green leaves on 'em."

Then Little Jim whisked on ahead of us, every now and then stopping to make rabbit tracks in the snow with his pretty striped ash stick.

Boy oh boy, I wished it was already spring, 'cause when spring came we could all go barefoot again. And as soon as Sugar Creek's face was thawed out, we'd go swimming in the old swimming hole and maybe have some very exciting brand new adventures, like we always do every spring and summer.

The first thing I wanted to do when spring came, was to go fishing.

I was thinking what fun it'd be when spring came, when all of a sudden I heard a roaring sound coming from the direction of Dragonfly's dad's woods, like a terrible wind was beginning to blow through the bare trees. I looked up quick and noticed that the sky in that direction was darkish looking and kind of brown, like there was a lot of dust blowing in from some faraway prairie. Then I felt a gust of cold wind hit me hard in the face.

In almost half a jiffy all of us were in a whirling snowstorm, and I knew the new cold wave had already come, and that before spring got to Sugar Creek we'd have a lot more winter—in fact there might even be a blizzard.

"Hurry up!" all of us yelled. "We've got to get home quick."

But that's the beginning of another Sugar Creek Gang story, which I hope I'll get a chance to write for you real soon.